THE PILGRIM'S PROGRESS

AN UNABRIDGED JOURNEY IN TODAY'S ENGLISH

BOOK 1: CHRISTIAN'S JOURNEY

JOHN BUNYAN

UNABRIDGED 1678 EDITION

UPDATED TO CONTEMPORARY
ENGLISH BY J.B. CYPRUS

First Edition

J. B. Cyprus

PO Box 30532

Houston, TX 77249

jbcyprus.com

Published in the United States by Jubilee Prison Ministry Press, The Woodlands, Texas.

Jubilee Prison Ministry Press

An imprint of Jubilee Prison Ministry, Inc.

2200 Lake Woodlands Dr.

The Woodlands, TX 77380

jubileeprisonministry.org

Paperback ISBN: 979-8-9907419-4-2

CONTENTS

Other Books From Jubilee Prison Ministry Press

Letters to Bentrock: A Demon's Guide to Trapping Prey

In the tradition of C.S. Lewis' classic work *The Screwtape Letters*, Lucifer's tempters pursue a new generation of "Prey" inside a Texas Prison.

A brilliant and satirical look at today's spiritual warfare—told through letters written by a Senior Tempter to a new, Junior Tempter under his tutelage.

The Evil One has updated and modernized his lies and temptations, but his objective is the same: steer one more soul onto the broad road that leads to his home Below.

Readers will find themselves immersed in this realistic look at how tempters cynically leverage the modern culture and our human weaknesses to pursue their prey, both in prison and in the "free world". Fortunately for our inmate, he is not alone in this fight. None of us are.

"*Letters to Bentrock* is, all at the same time, insightful, hilarious, serious and brilliant. The author has a keen understanding of the psychological and spiritual climate in a prison... Highly recommended." Dr. Vance Drum, former Head of Chaplaincy, Texas Department of Criminal Justice.

Letters to Bentrock: Small Group Study Guide

A study guide for individuals and small groups who would like to use *Letters to Bentrock* as a starting point to discuss the temptations and pitfalls we encounter as Christians in the modern world. This guide includes questions to encourage personal reflection, relevant Scripture references, and a weekly group discussion guide.

The Pilgrim's Progress Book 2: Christiana's Journey

Join our Pilgrims for Part 2 of this beloved and enduring adventure. As the 350th anniversary of its first publication approaches, this timeless allegory is ready to captivate and challenge a new generation of readers. This complete, unabridged 1684 edition has been thoughtfully translated into modern English for today's Christian journey.

Introduction

For more than three centuries, John Bunyan's *The Pilgrim's Progress* was, after the King James Bible, the second most read and influential work of Christian literature in the English language. Generations have turned to its timeless allegory to chart the believer's journey.

Yet in much of the modern West, Bunyan's tale is now often relegated to a children's cartoon, its depth and urgency overlooked. As we approach the 350th anniversary of its publication, it is my hope that this modern translation will make a minor contribution to restoring the book to its rightful place as a touchstone for Christian imagination and discipleship.

Of course, it is fair to ask: why another translation? Several fine modern versions of this classic exist. My goal was twofold. First, this unabridged edition is meant to be accessible and affordable—especially in ministry settings like those served by Jubilee Prison Ministry. We have set the retail pricing as low as we are able, and we are offering each book as a stand-alone volume, as Bunyan originally published them, as well as in a combined volume. (We are also making the text and illustrations available at no cost to non-profit ministry organizations that wish to reprint this.)

Second, Bunyan's work has been for me a deeply loved personal companion over these past decades. It has never been too far from my mind as my own understanding of temptation, grace, and Christian obedience has been forged on my journey through life (including a long and painful stint in Doubting Castle) and through my volunteer work in Texas prisons. It was also a central inspiration for my previous book, *Letters to Bentrock: A Demon's Guide to Trapping Prey*. In that work, which owes its style to C.S. Lewis's *The Screwtape Letters*, I explored the Deceiver's tactics within the context of a Texas prison. Where *Bentrock* examined the journey from the tempter's perspective, *The Pilgrim's Progress* illuminates it from the believer's. They have always seemed to me natural companions.

As we read this classic work it is important to remember that Bunyan was very much a man of a particular place and time. He was a rural

English working man, a traveling tinker who repaired pots and pans. His first wife, whose name is lost to history, brought to their marriage what Bunyan would come to realize was a dowry of inestimable worth: her devotion to the Lord and two books, *The Plain Man's Pathway to Heaven* and *The Practice of Piety*. It was the Lord working through this anonymous woman that transformed Bunyan from a self-centered rogue into the devout Nonconformist who would spend twelve years in prison for preaching outside the established Church of England. His theology can feel severe to modern readers, and his imagery is shaped by the medieval notions of heaven and hell still popular in his day. Yet beyond the coloring of time and place lies a profound and timeless insight into the human heart. Christian and Christiana's struggles at the Slough of Despond, their battles with the Giant Despair, their temptations and struggles are our own. Their journeys are our journey—and, to our surprise, three-and-a-half centuries on, Bunyan's world still looks very much like our own from Vanity Fair to Madame Bubbles the places and characters are the same.

This translation was a unique journey in itself, a collaboration between human and machine. The entire text was translated, paragraph by painstaking paragraph, in a running dialogue with Google's Gemini AI. Most of the illustrations that grace these pages were created with the help of ChatGPT. This project stands as a testament to how these new tools, guided by a clear purpose, can empower creativity and learning in unprecedented ways.

The Pilgrim's Progress Book 1 and Book 2 are the first in what we hope will be a new series, *Christian Classics for Today's Pilgrim*. We are looking forward to bringing other, lesser-known works of faith to a new audience if these are well received.

Ultimately, all of this—the translation, the art, the ministry it supports, and the journey it describes—is done for the glory of the Lord, who is the beginning and the end of every pilgrim's path.

— J. B. Cyprus

Houston, Texas

October 2025

About The Translation

I have set out to create a faithful and unabridged version of Bunyan's original, but as with any work of this sort, the translator's style, biases, and personality will color the final result. I have noted above that I made extensive use of AI (primarily Google Gemini) during the translation process. Since, as of this writing, these tools remain relatively new and less familiar to many readers, I thought it might be useful to share how the process worked (you may skip this if it is not of interest!).

I began by setting specific objectives for the project and I then fed the complete 1678 text from Gutenberg into Gemini along with examples of my previous writing to establish a target voice. Once we had "agreed" on some key general principals (like using NIV or ESV Bible translations in the text and using modern standard dialogue punctuation rather than Bunyan's screenplay style), we began the translation process.

Gemini would take a first pass at translating one or two paragraphs and present the proposed update and the original text side by side. I would then edit or rewrite its proposed text and send it back. Gemini would comment on my re-writes, either agreeing or disagreeing. (Often there was considerable back-and-forth about a theological point or an area of disagreement.)

We spent time exploring the history of archaic words like *pickthank* and words whose meaning had shifted significantly like *diffident.* Some of these discussions are distilled in the explanatory footnotes. When I disagreed or doubted Gemini's perspective, I would use an alternative AI as a fact checker (an often-annoying process since these models are designed to be over-eager conversational opinion givers and not dispassionate fact-checkers).

Once the entire first draft was complete, I submitted the entire manuscript to two other AI reviewers for feedback and suggestions, while also have a couple of humans re-read the entire translation. I then incorporated these consolidated review comments (some helpful, some not) in collaboration with the original Gemini assistant. Finally, I completed the layout of the book and identified spaces that could be usefully filled with illustrations while not bloating the page count. Armed with this, I spent a few days working with ChatGPT to create the illustrations you see here (color versions in the e-book).

The use of AI, in my estimation, accelerated the process at least four-fold. While the models remain very far from having the ability to "create a modern English translation" on their own, they are incredibly helpful collaborative tools.

I hope you find this translation acceptable and accessible. As always, I welcome comment or correction.

– JBC

Example of Bunyan's Original:

APOL. Consider, again, when thou art in cool blood, what thou art like to meet with in the way that thou goest. Thou knowest that, for the most part, his servants come to an ill end, because they are transgressors against me and my ways. How many of them have been put to shameful deaths! and, besides, thou countest his service better than mine, whereas he never came yet from the place where he is to deliver any that served him out of their hands; but as for me, how many times, as all the world very well knows, have I delivered, either by power, or fraud, those that have faithfully served me, from him and his, though taken by them; and so I will deliver thee.

Example of the updated version:

"Think again, when you have a clear head, about what you are likely to face on the path you are taking," Apollyon warned. "You know that most of His servants come to a bad end because they are rebels against me and my ways. How many of them have been put to shameful deaths! And besides, you consider His service better than mine, yet He has never come down to deliver even one of His servants from their enemies. But as for me, the world knows all too well the many times I have delivered—either by power or by trickery—those who have faithfully served me from Him and His followers, even after they were captured. I will deliver you in the same way."

The Author's Apology for his Book

When first I took my pen in hand
Thus for to write, I did not understand
That I at all would make a little book
Of this sort. No, I had undertook
To write another; which, when almost done,
Before I was aware, I this one'd begun.

And thus it was: I, writing of the way
And race of saints, in this our gospel day,
Fell suddenly into an allegory
About their journey, and the way to glory,

In more than twenty thoughts I wrote them down,
Then twenty more thoughts filled my crown,
And they again began to multiply,
Like sparks that from the coals of fire do fly.

"No, then," thought I, "if you breed so fast,
I'll set you by yourselves, lest you at last
Should grow unending, and crowd out
The book that I am already about."

Well, so I did; but yet I did not think
To show to all the world my pen and ink
In such a way; I only thought to make
I knew not what; nor did I undertake
Thereby to please my neighbor: no, not I;
I did it my own self to gratify.

Chapter 1: A Burden and a Dream

As I traveled through the wilderness of this world, I came to a place with a den[1] where I lay down to sleep. And as I slept, I had a dream. I dreamed I saw a man dressed in rags, standing with his back to his own house. He held a book in his hand and carried a heavy burden on his back.[a] I watched as he opened the book and read from it. While he read, he wept and trembled, and unable to contain himself any longer, he let out a sorrowful cry, asking, "What must I do?" [b]

In this state, he returned home and tried to hide his feelings for as long as he could, so that his wife and children wouldn't notice his distress. But as his anxiety grew, he couldn't stay silent for long. Finally, he revealed his thoughts to his wife and children, saying, "Oh, my dear wife, and you, my beloved children, I, your loving husband and father, am overwhelmed by a heavy burden that weighs on me. I have been told for certain that our city will be destroyed by fire from heaven, and in that terrible destruction we will all be miserably ruined, unless a way of escape can be found—which I do not yet see—so that we can be saved."

His family was greatly alarmed by this, not because they believed what he said was true, but because they thought he had gone mad! Therefore, as night approached, hoping that sleep would calm his mind, they quickly put him to bed. But the night was as restless for him as the day, and instead of sleeping, he spent it sighing and crying.

So, when morning came, they asked him how he was. He replied, "Worse and worse." He tried to talk to them again, but their hearts began to harden. They tried to cure his madness by treating him harshly; sometimes they would mock him, sometimes they would scold him, and at other times they would ignore him completely. Because of this, he began to withdraw to his room to pray for them and pity them, and also to lament his own misery. He would also walk alone in the fields,

---

[1] *In the 17th century, a "den" could refer to a humble lodging or private room, not just an animal's lair. It is a common interpretation that Bunyan uses it to establish the narrator's lowly and solitary state as he begins his dream.*

sometimes reading and sometimes praying, and this is how he spent his days.

Then I saw that one day, as he was walking in the fields, he was reading his book as usual, and his mind was deeply troubled. As he read, he burst out, just as he had before, crying, "What must I do to be saved?[c]"

I also saw him look this way and that, as if he wanted to run, yet he remained standing still because, as I could tell, he didn't know which way to go. Then I looked and saw a man named Evangelist approaching him, who asked, "Why are you crying out?"[d]

He answered, "Sir, I understand from the book in my hand that I am condemned to die, and after that to face judgment.[e] I find that I am not willing for the first,[f] and not able for the second.[g]"

Then Evangelist asked, "Why are you not willing to die, since this life is filled with so many troubles?"

The man answered, "Because I am afraid that this burden on my back will pull me down lower than the grave, and I will fall into **Hell.**[2h] And sir, if I am not fit to go to prison, I am certainly not fit to face judgment, and from there, execution. The thought of these things is what makes me cry out."

"If that is your situation," Evangelist said, "why are you just standing here?"

He replied, "Because I don't know where to go."

Then Evangelist handed him a parchment scroll and written on it were the words: "Flee from the wrath to come.[i]"

The man read the scroll and, looking carefully at Evangelist, asked, "Where must I flee?"

Evangelist pointed across a very wide field and said, "Do you see the small gate over there?[j]"

The man replied, "No."

Then Evangelist asked, "Do you see the shining light over there?[k]"

He said, "I think I do."

---

[2] *Bunyan's original word here is "Tophet," a real valley from the Old Testament that became a powerful poetic term for Hell. The translation uses "Hell" for modern clarity.*

Then Evangelist said, "Keep that light in your sight and go directly toward it, and you will see the gate. When you knock on it, you will be told what you must do."

So, I saw in my dream that the man began to run. He had not gone far from his own door when his wife and children saw him and began to cry out for him to return. But the man put his fingers in his ears and ran on, shouting, "Life! Life! Eternal life![l]" He did not look behind him but fled toward the middle of the plain.[m]

His neighbors also came out to see him run.[n] As he ran, some mocked him, others threatened him, and some shouted for him to come back. Among those who called after him, two were determined to bring him back by force. The name of the first was **Obstinate**, and the name of the second was **Pliable**. By this time, the man was a good distance away, but they were determined to chase him, which they did, and they soon caught up to him.

"Neighbors," the man said, "why have you come?"

They replied, "To persuade you to come back with us."

But he said, "That is impossible. You live in the **City of Destruction**—the same place where I was born. I see it for what it is. If you die there, sooner or later you will sink lower than the grave, into a place that burns with fire and brimstone. Be content, my good neighbors, and come with me."

"What!" exclaimed Obstinate, "And leave our friends and our comforts behind?"

Christian, for that was his name, replied, "Yes, because everything you would leave behind is not worthy to be compared with even a small part of what I am seeking to enjoy.[o] If you will come with me and endure, you will have the same as I will; for where I am going, there is more than enough.[p] Come with me and see if my words are true."

"What are these things you seek, that you would leave the whole world to find them?" asked Obstinate.

Christian replied confidently, "I seek an inheritance that is imperishable, unstained, and unfading.[q] It is kept safe in heaven, to be given at the appointed time to those who diligently seek it.[r] You can read it for yourself in my book, if you wish."

"Nonsense!" Obstinate scoffed. "Put that book away. Are you coming back with us or not?"

"No," Christian answered, "because I have put my hand to the plow.[s]"

"Come then, neighbor Pliable, let's turn around and go home without him," Obstinate said. "There is a whole group of these crackpots who, once they get an idea in their heads, think they are wiser than seven reasonable men.[t]"

But Pliable said, "Don't insult him. If what good Christian says is true, the things he is seeking are better than ours. My heart is leaning toward going with him."

"What, another fool?" Obstinate snapped. "Listen to me and go back! Who knows where a madman like this will lead you? Go back, go back, and be wise."

"No, come with me, Pliable," Christian urged. "The things I spoke of are real, and there are many more glories besides. If you don't believe me, read it here in this book. And as for the truth of what it says, it is all confirmed by the blood of Him who wrote it.[u]"

"Well, neighbor Obstinate," Pliable said, "I'm starting to make up my mind. I'm going to go with this good man and cast my lot in with him." Turning to Christian he asked, "Do you know the way to this place we desire?"

"I was told by a man named Evangelist to hurry to a small gate up ahead of us," Christian explained. "There, we will receive instructions about the way."

"Come then, good neighbor, let's be on our way," said Pliable. And so they went on together.

"And I will go back to my own place," Obstinate grumbled. "I will not be a companion to such deluded and fanciful fools."

Now I saw in my dream that after Obstinate had gone back, Christian and Pliable walked on, talking as they crossed the plain. This is how their conversation began.

"Come, neighbor Pliable, how are you?" Christian began. "I am glad you were persuaded to come with me. If Obstinate had only felt what I have felt of the power and terror of the unseen world, he wouldn't have turned his back on us so easily."

"Come, neighbor Christian," Pliable said, "since it's just the two of us here, tell me more about the things we are seeking, and how we will enjoy them when we get where we are going."

"I can imagine them better in my mind than I can describe them with my tongue," Christian replied. "But since you want to know, I will read about them from my book."

"And do you think that the words in your book are absolutely true?" asked Pliable.

"Yes, truly," Christian answered, "for it was written by Him who cannot lie.[v]"

"Well said. What are these things?" Pliable asked.

Christian replied, "There is an endless kingdom for us to live in, and we will be given everlasting life so that we may live in that kingdom forever[w]."

"That's wonderful," Pliable said. "What else?"

"There are crowns of glory to be given to us," Christian continued, "and clothes that will make us shine like the sun in the sky.[x]"

"This is very pleasant," Pliable remarked. "And what else?"

"There will be no more crying or sorrow, for the one who owns that place will wipe away all tears from our eyes.[y]"

"And what kind of company will we have there?" Pliable asked.

Christian answered, "There we will be with seraphim and cherubim, creatures so dazzling they will astound you.[z] You will also meet with thousands and tens of thousands who have gone before us to that place.[aa] None of them are harmful; they are all loving and holy, each one walking in the sight of God and standing in His presence, accepted forever. In short, we will see the elders with their golden crowns,[bb] the holy virgins with their golden harps,[cc] and we will see people who, for the love of the Lord of that place, were cut to pieces, burned in flames, devoured by beasts, or drowned in the seas—all of them restored and clothed with immortality.[dd]"

"Just hearing about this is enough to thrill one's heart!" Pliable exclaimed. "But are these things truly for us to enjoy? How can we share in them?"

Christian answered, "The Lord, the Governor of that country, has written in this book that if we are truly willing to have it, He will give it to us freely."

"Well, my good companion, I am glad to hear of these things," said Pliable. "Come on, let's hurry!"

"I cannot go as fast as I would like," Christian said, "because of this burden on my back."

Now I saw in my dream that just as they finished this conversation, they drew near a very muddy swamp in the middle of the plain. Being careless, they both fell suddenly into the bog. The name of the swamp was **Despond**. There they struggled for a while, covered in filth. And Christian, because of the burden on his back, began to sink in the mire.

Then Pliable cried out, "Ah, neighbor Christian, where are you now?"

"Truly," said Christian, "I do not know."

At that, Pliable became offended and said angrily to his companion, "Is this the happiness you've been telling me about all this time? If we have such bad luck at the very start of our journey, what can we expect between here and the end? If I can just get out of here with my life, you can have that fine country all to yourself."

And with that, he gave one or two desperate struggles and pulled himself out of the mud on the side of the swamp that was closest to his own house. Then he left, and Christian never saw him again.

So Christian was left to struggle alone in the **Slough of Despond**. He still tried to fight his way to the side of the swamp that was farther from his own house and closer to the small gate. He managed to get there, but he could not pull himself out because of the burden on his back.

But I saw in my dream that a man whose name was **Help** came to him and asked, "What are you doing here?"

"Sir," Christian said, "I was told to go this way by a man named Evangelist, who also directed me to the gate over there so that I might escape the coming wrath. As I was on my way, I fell in here."

"But why didn't you look for the steps?" Help asked.

"I was in such a hurry that I was running and fell in," Christian admitted.

"Then give me your hand," he said. So Christian gave him his hand, and Help pulled him out, setting him on solid ground and telling him to continue on his way.[ee]

Then I stepped toward the one who had pulled him out and asked, "Sir, since this is the main path from the City of Destruction to the gate over there, why isn't this patch of ground fixed so that poor travelers might have an easier journey?"

Help explained, "This muddy swamp is the kind of place that cannot be fixed. It is the low ground where all the scum and filth that comes with the conviction of sin collects, and that is why it is called the Slough of Despond. For as a sinner awakens to his lost condition, many fears, doubts, and discouraging thoughts arise in his soul, and they all gather and settle in this place. This is what makes the ground so bad."

"It is not the King's will that this place should remain so bad,[ff]" Help continued. "For more than sixteen hundred years, his laborers have been working on this patch of ground, following the directions of his surveyors, to see if it could be fixed. Yes, and to my knowledge," he said, "at least twenty thousand cartloads—truly, millions—of wholesome instructions have been brought from all over the King's dominions and dumped here in every season. Those who know say this is the best material for making the ground solid, but despite all that, it is still the Slough of Despond, and it will remain so after they have done all they can."

"It is true," he went on, "that by the Lawgiver's direction, there are some good and sturdy steps placed right through the middle of this swamp. But when this place spews out its filth, as it does when the weather changes, these steps are hard to see. Or, if they can be seen, people, in their dizziness, step aside and get stuck in the mud, even though the steps are there. But the ground is good once you get through the gate.[gg]"

Now I saw in my dream that by this time Pliable had returned to his house. His neighbors came to visit him; some called him a wise man for coming back, while others called him a fool for risking himself with Christian. Still others mocked his cowardice, saying, "Surely, after starting the adventure, I wouldn't have been so shameful as to give up after only a few difficulties." So Pliable sat among them, ashamed. But eventually, he regained his confidence, and then they all changed their stories and began to ridicule poor Christian behind his back. And that is all there is to say about Pliable.

Now, as Christian was walking alone, he saw someone in the distance crossing the field to meet him, and they happened to meet just as their paths crossed. The gentleman's name was **Mr. Worldly Wiseman**[3]. He lived in the town of **Carnal Policy**, a very large town not far from where Christian had come.

This man, upon meeting Christian, had some idea of who he was, for Christian's departure from the City of Destruction was widely talked about, not only in his own town but in the surrounding areas as well. He began to strike up a conversation.

"Hello there, good fellow," Mr. Worldly Wiseman said. "Where are you going in such a burdened state?"

"A burdened state indeed," Christian replied, "as burdened as I think any poor creature has ever been! And as for your question of where I am going, I tell you, sir, I am going to the small gate up ahead. For I have been told that there I will be shown the way to get rid of my heavy burden."

"Do you have a wife and children?" Mr. Worldly Wiseman asked.

"Yes," said Christian, "but I am so weighed down by this burden that I cannot enjoy them as I used to. It feels as if I have none.[hh]"

"Will you listen to me if I give you some advice?" Mr. Worldly Wiseman inquired.

"If it is good advice, I will," Christian answered, "for I am in great need of it."

"I would advise you, then," Mr. Worldly Wiseman began, "to get rid of your burden. I can tell you how to do it without going to that gate over there, where you are likely to face so many difficulties."

"Please, sir, tell me this secret," said Christian.

---

[3] *A common interpretation is that Mr. Worldly Wiseman and his town, "Carnal Policy," represent the temptation to solve spiritual problems using worldly wisdom and practical strategies ("policy") rather than by relying on God's revealed path. "Carnal" here means "of the flesh" or "worldly."*

"Why, in that village over there—the village is named **Morality**—lives a gentleman whose name is **Legality**," he explained. "He is a very wise man with a good reputation who is skilled at helping men remove burdens like yours from their shoulders. To my knowledge, he has done a great deal of good in this way. And besides that, he has the skill to cure those who have been driven a little mad by their burdens. You may go to him, as I said, and be helped immediately. His house is not even a mile from here. If he isn't home himself, he has a fine young son named **Civility**, who can do the job just as well as the old gentleman himself."

He continued, "There, I say, you can be relieved of your burden. And if you don't want to return to your former home—and indeed, I wouldn't advise it—you can send for your wife and children to join you in this village. There are empty houses there now, one of which you can have for a reasonable price. The food is also cheap and good. And what will make your life even happier is that you will live among honest, respectable neighbors in good standing."

Now Christian was at a loss, but he soon concluded, "If what this gentleman has said is true, my wisest course is to take his advice." And with that, he spoke again.

"Sir, which way is it to this honest man's house?" Christian asked.

"Do you see that high hill over there?" Mr. Worldly Wiseman replied.

"Yes, very well."

"You must go by that hill," he instructed, "and the first house you come to is his."

So, Christian turned from his path to go to Mr. Legality's house for help. But when he got close to the hill, it seemed so high, and the side of it next to the road hung over so much, that Christian was afraid to go any farther, fearing the hill would fall on his head. So, he stood there, not knowing what to do. His burden now seemed heavier to him than it had on his original path. Flashes of fire also shot out from the hill, making Christian fear he would be burned.[ii] He began to sweat and tremble with fear,[jj] and he was sorry he had taken Mr. Worldly Wiseman's advice.

Just then, he saw Evangelist coming to meet him, and the sight of him made Christian blush with shame. Evangelist drew closer and closer, and when he reached him, he looked at him with a severe and fearsome expression and began to question him.

---

[a] *Isa. 64:6; Luk. 14:33; Psa. 38:4; Hab. 2:2; Act. 16:30-31*
[b] *Act. 2:37*
[c] *Act. 16:30-31*
[d] *Job. 33:23*
[e] *Heb. 9:27*
[f] *Job. 16:21*
[g] *Eze. 22:14*
[h] *Isa. 30:33*
[i] *Mat. 3:7*
[j] *Mat. 7:13-14*
[k] *Psa. 119:105; 2 Pe 1:19*
[l] *Luk. 14:26*
[m] *Gen. 19:17*
[n] *Jer. 20:10*
[o] *2Co. 4:18*
[p] *Luk. 15:17*
[q] *1Pe. 1:4*
[r] *Heb. 11:16*
[s] *Luk. 9:62*
[t] *Pro. 26:16*
[u] *Heb. 9:17-22; Heb 13:20*
[v] *Tit. 1:2*
[w] *Isa. 45:17; Jhn 10:28-29*
[x] *2Ti. 4:8; Rev 3:4; Mat 13:43*
[y] *Isa. 25:6-8; Rev 7:17; Rev 21:4*
[z] *Isa. 6:2*
[aa] *1Th. 4:16-17; Rev 5:11*
[bb] *Rev. 4:4*
[cc] *Rev. 14:1-5*
[dd] *Jhn. 12:25; 2 Co 5:4*
[ee] *Psa. 40:2*
[ff] *Isa. 35:3-4*
[gg] *1Sa. 12:23*
[hh] *1Co. 7:29*
[ii] *Exo. 19:16-18*
[jj] *Heb. 12:21*

Chapter 2: A Severe Rebuke and the Path Rediscovered

When Christians heed a worldly ear,
They leave the path and pay most dear;
For Worldly Wiseman can but steer
A saint to bondage and to fear.

"What are you doing here, Christian?" he asked. At these words, Christian knew it was Evangelist. He blushed with shame. Evangelist continued, "Are you not the man I found crying outside the walls of the City of Destruction?"

"Yes, dear sir, I am," Christian replied.

"Did I not direct you to the way of the small wicket-gate?" Evangelist pressed.

"Yes, dear sir, you did," Christian admitted.

"How is it, then, that you have turned aside so quickly?" Evangelist asked. "For you are now off the path."

"He looked like a gentleman, and he was very convincing. In the end, he persuaded me," Christian said. "So I came here. But when I saw this cliff and how it hangs over the road, I stopped suddenly, afraid it might fall on my head if I continue."

Evangelist asked sharply, "What did that gentleman say to you?"

"Well, he asked me where I was going, and I told him," Christian answered.

"And what did he say then?"

"He asked if I had a family, and I told him I did. 'But,' I said, 'I am so weighed down by this burden on my back that I cannot enjoy them as I used to.'"

"And what did he say then?"

"He told me to get rid of my burden quickly, and I told him that relief was what I was looking for. He said, 'I will show you a better, shorter way, one not so full of difficulties as the way, sir, that you put me on.' He said his way would lead me to a gentleman's house who had the skill to take these burdens off. So I believed him and turned from that path onto this one, hoping to be relieved of my burden quickly. But when I came to this place and saw how things were, I stopped for fear of the danger, as I said. And now I don't know what to do."

Then Evangelist commanded, "Stand still for a moment, so that I may show you the words of God." So, Christian stood there, trembling. Then Evangelist said, "'See to it that you do not refuse Him who speaks. For if they did not escape when they refused Him who spoke on earth, how much less will we escape if we turn away from Him who speaks from heaven.[a]'" He also quoted, "'Now the just shall live by faith; but if anyone draws back, My soul has no pleasure in him.[b]'" He also applied the saying, "'You are snared by the words of your mouth; you are taken by the words of your mouth.'" At this, Christian fell at his feet as if dead, crying out, "Woe is me, for I am ruined!"

At this sight, Evangelist caught him by the right hand and said, "All kinds of sin and blasphemy will be forgiven.[c] Do not be faithless but believe.[d]" Then Christian revived a little and stood up trembling before Evangelist, just as he had at first.

Evangelist continued, saying, "Pay close attention to the things I am about to tell you. I will now show you who it was that deceived you, and also who it was he sent you to.

The man who met you is named **Mr. Worldly Wiseman**, and he is rightly called that, partly because he only savors the teachings of this world[e]—which is why he always goes to church in the town of Morality—and partly because he loves that teaching best, for it saves him from the cross. And because he has this worldly mindset, he tries to corrupt my teachings, though they are right." [f]

"Now, there are three things in this man's advice that you must utterly hate.

His turning you from the path.

His effort to make the cross offensive to you.

And his setting your feet on the path that leads to the **ministry of death.**"[1]

"First, you must hate that he turned you from the path, and you must also hate that you consented to it, because this is to reject the counsel of God for the sake of the counsel of a Worldly Wiseman. The Lord says,

---

[1] *A theological term from the New Testament (2 Corinthians 3:7) for the Law of Moses. The common interpretation is that the Law, while holy, can only reveal sin and its deadly consequences; it has no power to save.*

'Strive to enter through the narrow gate'—the gate to which I sent you—'for narrow is the gate and difficult is the way which leads to life, and there are few who find it.[g]' This wicked man has turned you away from this small gate, and from the way that leads to it, nearly bringing you to destruction. Therefore, hate him for turning you from the path, and hate yourself for listening to him."

"Second, you must hate his effort to make the cross offensive to you. You are to prefer the way of the cross 'more than the treasures of Egypt.[h]' Besides, the King of Glory has told you that whoever 'wishes to save his life will lose it.[i]' And, 'If anyone comes to Me and does not hate his father and mother, wife and children, brothers and sisters, yes, and his own life also, he cannot be My disciple.[j]' Therefore, I say, if any man comes to you and tries to set you against the cross by telling you that this way is full of difficulties, you must consider him an enemy. You must watch, and pray, and get away from him, so that you are not corrupted by his errors."

"Third, you must hate that he set your feet on the path that leads to the ministry of death. For this, you must consider who he sent you to, and also how unable that person was to deliver you from your burden.

The one he sent you to for relief is named **Legality**, a son of the slave woman who is now in slavery with her children.[k] He represents this Mount Sinai, which you feared would fall on your head. Now, if she and her children are in slavery, how can you expect them to make you free? This Legality, therefore, cannot set you free from your burden. He has never relieved any man of his burden and he never will. You cannot be justified by the works of the law! No living person can cast off his burden through deeds of the law. Therefore, Mr. Worldly Wiseman is a foreigner to the faith, Mr. Legality is a cheat, and as for his son, Civility, despite his smug smile, he is just a hypocrite who cannot help you. Believe me, everything these foolish men have said is nothing but a plot to cheat you out of your salvation by turning you from the path on which I had set you."

After this, Evangelist called out to the heavens for confirmation of what he had said. With that, words and fire came from the mountain under which poor Christian stood, making the hair on his skin stand up.

The words were pronounced, 'For all who rely on the works of the law are under a curse, as it is written: Cursed is everyone who does not continue to do everything written in the Book of the Law.[l]'

Now Christian expected nothing but death and began to cry out pitifully, cursing the moment he met Mr. Worldly Wiseman and calling himself the greatest of fools for listening to his advice. He was deeply ashamed to think that this man's arguments, coming only from a worldly perspective, could have had such a strong effect on him as to make him abandon the right path. When he had finished, he turned again to Evangelist and spoke to him as follows:

"Sir, what do you think? Is there any hope? May I return to the path and head to the wicket-gate? Will I be rejected for this and sent away from there in shame? I am so sorry I listened to this man's advice. But can my sin be forgiven?"

Then Evangelist said to him, "Your sin is very great: you have abandoned the good way to walk on forbidden paths. Yet the man at the gate will receive you, for he has goodwill for all mankind. Only," he said, "be careful that you do not turn aside again, 'lest something worse happen to you.[m]'" Then Christian prepared himself to go back, and Evangelist, after he had kissed him, gave him a smile and wished him Godspeed.

---

[a] *Heb. 12:25*
[b] *Heb. 10:38*
[c] *Mat. 12:31; Mrk 3:28*
[d] *Jhn. 20:27*
[e] *1 Jhn. 4:5*
[f] *Gal. 6:12*
[g] *Luk. 13:24; Mat 7:14*
[h] *Heb. 11:25-26*
[i] *Mrk. 8:35; Jhn 12:25; Mat 10:39*
[j] *Luk. 14:26*
[k] *Gal. 4:21-27*
[l] *Gal. 3:10*
[m] *Psa. 2:12*

Chapter 3: The Gate and the House of the Interpreter

The one who wants to enter must first stand
Outside the gate and knock with steady hand,
Before a welcome he can hope to see,
Or, once let in, be truly welcomed be.

So Christian hurried on, not speaking to anyone along the road; nor would he give an answer if anyone asked him a question. He walked like someone treading on forbidden ground and could not think of himself as safe until he was back on the path he had left to follow Mr. Worldly Wiseman's advice.

In time, Christian arrived at the gate. Over it was written, "Knock, and it shall be opened to you.[a]" He knocked, therefore, several times and each time saying:

"May I now enter here? Will He within, Open to wretched me, though I have been An undeserving rebel? Then I will Not fail to sing His lasting praise still."

At last, a serious-looking person named **Goodwill**[1] came to the gate and asked who was there, where he came from, and what he wanted.

"I am a poor, burdened sinner," Christian answered. "I have come from the City of Destruction and am going to Mount Zion, so that I may be delivered from the wrath to come. Since I have been told that this gate is the way there, I would like to know, sir, if you are willing to let me in."

"I am willing with all my heart," he said, and with that, he opened the gate.

As Christian began to step through the gate, the other man grabbed him and quickly pulled him through.

---

[1] *It is a common interpretation that* ***Goodwill*** *represents* ***Jesus Christ****, who welcomes all who come to him at the entrance to the path of faith.*

"Why did you grab me?" Christian asked.

The other man told him, "A short distance from this gate, a strong castle has been built, and its captain is Beelzebub. From there, he and his soldiers shoot arrows at those who come up to this gate, hoping they might die before they can enter."

Then Christian said, "I rejoice and I tremble." After he was safely inside, the man asked Christian who had directed him there.

"Evangelist told me to come here and knock, as I did," Christian explained. "And he said that you, sir, would tell me what I must do."

"An open door is set before you, and no one can shut it," Goodwill replied.

"Now I begin to reap the benefits of my trials," Christian said.

"But how is it that you came alone?" Goodwill asked.

"Because none of my neighbors saw their danger as I saw mine."

"Did any of them know you were coming here?"

"Yes, my wife and children saw me leave at first and called after me to turn back," Christian said. "Also, some of my neighbors stood shouting and calling for me to return, but I put my fingers in my ears and continued on my way."

"But did none of them follow you to persuade you to go back?"

"Yes, both Obstinate and Pliable did," Christian answered. "But when they saw they could not succeed, Obstinate went back cursing, but Pliable came with me for a little while."

"But why didn't he come all the way?" Goodwill asked.

"We were traveling together until we came to the Slough of Despond, and we both suddenly fell in," Christian explained. "After that, my neighbor Pliable was discouraged and wouldn't risk going any farther. So, after getting out on the side closest to his own house, he told me I could have that fine country for myself. He went his way, and I came mine—he followed Obstinate, and I came to this gate."

"Alas, poor man," Goodwill said sadly. "Does he have so little appreciation for eternal glory that he doesn't consider it worth risking a few difficulties to obtain it?"

Christian cast his eyes to the ground and then began to speak once more: "I have told the truth about Pliable, but if I were to tell the whole truth about myself, it would be clear there is little difference between us," he sighed. "It's true that he went back to his own house, but I also turned aside to go down the way of death, persuaded by the worldly arguments of Mr. Worldly Wiseman."

"Oh, did he find you?" Goodwill exclaimed. "I suppose he wanted you to seek relief from Mr. Legality? They are both complete frauds. But did you take his advice?"

"Yes, as far as I dared," Christian confessed. "I went to find Mr. Legality, but I stopped when I thought the mountain that stands by his house was about to fall on my head."

"That mountain has been the death of many and will be the death of many more," Goodwill said. "It is a good thing you escaped being dashed to pieces by it."

"I don't know what would have become of me there if Evangelist hadn't met me again while I was lost in my despair," Christian replied. "It was God's mercy that he came to me again, otherwise I would have never made it here. But now I have come, a man like me, who is more deserving of death by that mountain than to be standing here talking with my Lord. Oh, what a kindness it is that I have been allowed to enter!"

"We do not bar anyone from entering this gate, regardless of what they have done before they came here. They are 'by no means cast out,[b]'" Goodwill said. "And so, good Christian, come a little way with me, and I will show you the path you must take."

Christian followed Goodwill and together they looked out toward the horizon beyond the gate. "Look ahead of you," said Goodwill, "do you see this narrow way? THAT is the path you must follow. It was established by the patriarchs, prophets, Christ, and His apostles, and it is as straight as a ruler can make it. This is the way you must go."

"But," asked Christian, "are there no turns or twists where a stranger might lose his way?"

"Yes, there are many paths that meet this one, and they are crooked and wide," Goodwill answered. "But this is how you can tell the right from the wrong: only the right way is straight and narrow.[c]"

Then I saw in my dream that Christian asked him if he could help him get rid of the burden on his back, for he had not gotten rid of it yet, and there was no way he could get it off without help.

The Interpreter

He told him, "As for your burden, be content to carry it until you come to the place of deliverance, for there it will fall from your back by itself."

Then Christian prepared himself to continue his journey. Goodwill explained that he would need to continue on the path for some distance and then he would come to the house of the **Interpreter**[2]. He should knock on the door, and the Interpreter would show him excellent things. Then Christian took leave of his friend, and Goodwill again wished him Godspeed.

He went on until he came to the house of the Interpreter, where he knocked over and over. At last, someone came to the door and asked who was there.

---

[a] *Mat. 7:8*
[b] *Jhn. 6:37*
[c] *Mat. 7:14*

---

[2] *The Interpreter is widely understood to represent the Holy Spirit, whose role is to teach and illuminate the truths of the faith for the believer through the allegorical visions shown in his house.*

Chapter 4: The House of the Interpreter

Here Christian sees his own life's story told
Through many symbols, precious truths unfold;
He learns to watch and walk with wiser feet,
And where to find his help in times of need.

"Sir," Christian said, "I am a traveler who was told by an acquaintance of the master of this house to call here for my own benefit. Therefore, I would like to speak with the master of the house."

So the servant called for the master of the house, who came to Christian after a little while and asked him what he wanted.

"Sir," said Christian, "I am a man who has come from the City of Destruction, and I am going to Mount Zion. I was told by Goodwill, who stands at the gate at the start of this path, that if I called here, you would show me excellent things that would help me on my journey."

"Come in," the Interpreter said. "I will show you what will be helpful to you." He commanded his servant to light a candle and told Christian to follow him.

He led him first into a private room and told his servant to open a door. When he had done so, Christian saw the portrait of a very serious person hanging on the wall. This is what it looked like: His eyes were lifted up to heaven, he held the best of books in his hand, the law of truth was written on his lips, and the world was behind his back. He stood as if he were pleading with people, and a crown of gold hung over his head.

"What does this mean?" Christian asked.

The Interpreter answered, "The man in this portrait is one in a thousand. He can father children,[a] labor in childbirth with them,[b] and nurse them himself when they are born. The fact that you see him with his eyes lifted to heaven, the best of books in his hand, and the law of truth written on his lips is to show you that his work is to understand and reveal deep truths to sinners. You also see him standing as if he is pleading with mankind. And the fact that you see the world cast behind him and a crown hanging over his head is to show you that by disregarding and despising the things of the present for the love he has for his Master's service, he is certain to have glory as his reward in the world to come."

"Now," said the Interpreter, "I have shown you this portrait first because the man it represents is the only one whom the Lord of the place where you are going has authorized to be your guide in all the difficult places you may encounter on your way. Therefore, pay close attention to what I have shown you, and keep what you have seen firmly in your mind, so that on your journey you do not follow some who pretend to lead you correctly, but whose way leads down to death."

Then he took him by the hand and led him into a very large room that was full of dust because it had never been swept. After Christian had looked at it for a little while, the Interpreter called for a man to sweep it. When the man began to sweep, the dust began to fly about so thickly that Christian was almost choked by it. Then the Interpreter said to a young woman standing nearby, "Bring water here and sprinkle the room." After she had done this, the room was swept and cleansed with ease.

"What does this mean?" Christian asked.

The Interpreter answered, "This room is the heart of a person who has never been sanctified by the sweet grace of the Gospel. The dust is his original sin and internal corruption, which has defiled the whole person. The man who began to sweep at first is the Law, and the young woman who brought water and sprinkled it is the Gospel. Now, you saw that as soon as the first one began to sweep, the dust flew about so much that the room could not be cleansed by him, and you were almost choked by it. This is to show you that the Law, instead of cleansing the heart from sin, actually revives sin, gives it strength, and increases it in the soul, even as it exposes and forbids it, because the Law does not give the power to conquer it.[c]"

"Again, you saw the young woman sprinkle the room with water, after which it was cleansed with pleasure. This is to show you that when the Gospel comes into the heart with its sweet and precious influence, then—just as you saw the young woman settle the dust by sprinkling the floor with water—sin is conquered and subdued. The soul is made clean through faith in the Gospel and, as a result, becomes fit for the King of glory to live in.[d]"

I saw, moreover, in my dream that the Interpreter took him by the hand and led him into a small room where two little children were sitting, each in his own chair. The name of the older one was **Passion**, and the name of the other was **Patience**. Passion seemed very discontented, but Patience was very quiet. Then Christian asked, "Why is Passion so discontented?" The Interpreter answered, "Their guardian wants him to wait for his best things until the beginning of next year, but he wants them all now. Patience, however, is willing to wait."

Then I saw someone come to Passion and bring him a bag of treasure, which was poured out at his feet. He picked it up and rejoiced in it, and he began to laugh at Patience with scorn. But I watched for only a little while before he had wasted it all away and had nothing left but rags.

Then Christian said to the Interpreter, "Explain what happened here more fully."

So he said, "These two boys are figures. Passion represents the people of this world, and Patience represents the people of the world that is to come. As you see here, Passion wants everything now, this year—that is to say, in this world. So it is with the people of this world: they must have all their good things now. They cannot wait until next year—that is, until the next world—for their portion of good. The proverb, 'A bird in the hand is worth two in the bush,' has more authority with them than all the divine promises of the good things in the world to come. But just as you saw that he quickly wasted everything and was soon left with nothing but rags, so it will be with all such people at the end of this world."

Then Christian said, "Now I see that Patience has the better wisdom, and for many reasons. First, because he waits for the best things. And second, because he will still have his glory when the other has nothing."

"No, you can add another reason," said the Interpreter. "The glory of the next world will never wear out, but these worldly things are gone in an instant. Therefore, Passion did not have as much reason to laugh at Patience for getting his good things first, as Patience will have to laugh at Passion for getting his best things last. For the first must give way to the last, because the last is still to come. But the last does not give way to the first, because there is nothing to follow it. He, therefore, who has his portion first, has only a limited time to spend it; but he who has his portion last will have it forever. That is why it is said of the rich man, 'In your lifetime you received your good things, while Lazarus received bad things, but now he is comforted here, and you are in agony.[e]'"

"Then I understand it is best not to desire the things of the present, but to wait for the things that are to come," Christian said.

"You speak the truth," the Interpreter replied, "'For what is seen is temporary, but what is unseen is eternal.[f]' But even though this is true, because present things and our earthly desires are such close neighbors, and because future things and our worldly senses are such strangers to one another, the first two quickly become friends while the second two remain distant."

Then I saw in my dream that the Interpreter took Christian by the hand and led him to a place where a fire was burning against a wall. Someone was standing beside it, constantly throwing great amounts of water on it to put it out, yet the fire only burned higher and hotter.

"What does this mean?" Christian asked.

The Interpreter answered, "This fire is the work of grace that is active in the heart. The one who throws water on it to extinguish it is the Devil. As for why you see the fire burn higher and hotter despite this, come with me."

So, he led Christian around to the back of the wall, where he saw a man with a container of oil in his hand, from which he was continually (but secretly) pouring into the fire.

"What does this mean?" Christian asked.

The Interpreter answered, "This is Christ, who, with the oil of His grace, continually maintains the work that has already begun in the heart. Because of this, despite everything the devil can do, the souls of His people continue to be filled with fire for the Lord.[g] And the fact that you saw the man standing behind the wall to maintain the fire is to teach you that it is difficult for a tempted person to see how this work of grace is kept alive in the soul."

I also saw that the Interpreter took him again by the hand and led him to a pleasant place where a stately and beautiful palace had been built. Christian was greatly delighted at the sight of it. He also saw, on the top of the palace, several people walking, and they were all clothed in gold.

"May we go inside?" Christian asked.

The Interpreter then led him up toward the door of the palace. At the door stood a great crowd of people who were eager to go in but did not dare. A little distance from the door, a man sat at a small table with a book and an inkwell before him to write down the name of anyone who would enter. He also saw that in the doorway stood many men in armor to guard it, determined to do as much harm and mischief as they could to anyone who tried to enter.

Christian was puzzled by this. At last, as everyone else was shrinking back in fear of the armed men, Christian saw a pilgrim with a very determined expression come up to the man who sat writing and say, "Set down my name, sir." After this was done, he saw the man draw his sword, put a helmet on his head, and rush toward the door to fight the armed men, who attacked him with deadly force. But the pilgrim, not at all discouraged, began cutting and hacking most fiercely. So after he had received and given many wounds to those who tried to keep him out, he cut his way through them all and pressed forward into the palace.[h]

At that, a pleasant voice was heard from those inside, from the ones walking on the top of the palace, saying:

"Come in, come in; Eternal glory you shall win."

So he went in and was clothed in garments like theirs. Then Christian smiled and said, "I believe I know the meaning of this."

"Now, let me go on from here," said Christian.

"No, stay," said the Interpreter, "until I have shown you a little more. After that, you may go on your way." So he took him by the hand again and led him into a very dark room, where a man sat in an iron cage.[1]

The man appeared to be very sad. He sat with his eyes looking down at the ground and his hands folded together, and he sighed as if his heart would break. "What does this mean?" Christian asked. At that, the Interpreter told him to talk with the man himself.

Then Christian said to the man, "Who are you?"

The man answered, "I am not who I once was."

"Who were you once?" Christian asked.

---

111 The man in an iron cage is a powerful image that, according to scholars, represents the Puritan understanding of apostasy—the state of a person who has willfully turned from grace and is trapped in a despair so profound that they believe repentance is no longer possible.

"I was once a thriving and respected believer, both in my own eyes and in the eyes of others,[i]" the man said. "I once believed I was destined for the Celestial City and even felt joy at the thought that I would get there."

"Well, but what are you now?"

"I am now a man trapped by my own despair. I am locked up in it, and I cannot get out. Oh, I cannot!"

"But how did you come to be in this condition?" Christian asked.

"I stopped being watchful and sober," the man explained. "I gave free rein to my lusts. I sinned against the light of the Word and the goodness of God. I have grieved the Spirit, and He is gone. I tempted the devil, and he has come to me. I have provoked God to anger, and He has left me. I have so hardened my heart that I cannot repent."

Then Christian asked, "But is there no hope for you?"

"No, none at all," the man replied.

"Why not? The Son of the Blessed is very merciful."

"I have crucified Him to myself all over again,[j]" he said. "I have despised His person[k], I have despised His righteousness, I have 'treated as an unholy thing the blood of the covenant,' and I have 'insulted the Spirit of grace.[l]' Therefore, I have shut myself out from all the promises, and now nothing remains for me but threats—dreadful threats, faithful threats of a certain judgment and a fiery indignation that will devour me as an enemy."

"Why did you allow yourself to fall into this condition?" Christian asked.

"For the lusts, pleasures, and profits of this world," he answered. "In enjoying them, I promised myself much delight. But now, every one of those things bites me and gnaws at me like a burning worm."

"But can you not repent and turn back now?" Christian asked.

"God has denied me repentance. His Word gives me no encouragement to believe. Indeed, He Himself has shut me up in this iron cage, and not all the people in the world can let me out. Oh, eternity! Eternity! How will I ever cope with the misery that I must face in eternity!"

Then the Interpreter said to Christian, "Let this man's misery be a permanent warning to you."

"This is terrifying," Christian said. "God help me to be watchful and sober, and to pray that I may avoid the cause of this man's misery. But now, let's continue."

"No, let us go to another place," the Interpreter corrected.

So he took Christian by the hand again and led him into a bedroom, where a man was getting out of bed. As he put on his clothes, he shook and trembled.

"Why does this man tremble so?" Christian asked.

The Interpreter then told the man to explain the reason for his trembling to Christian.

So the man began his story. "Last night, while I was asleep, I had a dream. The heavens grew completely black. It also thundered and lightninged in the most terrifying way, which put me in agony. I looked up in my dream and saw the clouds moving at an unusual speed. Then I heard the great sound of a trumpet and saw a man sitting on a cloud, accompanied by thousands from heaven. They were all in flaming fire, and the heavens themselves were a burning flame. I then heard a voice say, 'Arise, you dead, and come to judgment![m]' With that, the rocks split, the graves were opened, and the dead who were in them came out. Some of them were overjoyed and looked upward, while others tried to hide under the mountains.[n]

Then I saw the man who sat on the cloud open the book and command the world to draw near. Yet, because of a fiery flame that shot out from before him, there was a significant distance between him and them, like the distance between a judge and the prisoners at the bar.[o] I also heard it proclaimed to those who served the man on the cloud, 'Gather the weeds, the chaff, and the stubble, and throw them into the burning lake.[p]' And with that, the bottomless pit opened right near where I was standing. Out of its mouth came an enormous amount of smoke and coals of fire, with hideous noises. It was also said to the same servants, 'Gather my wheat into the barn.[q]' And with that, I saw many people caught up and carried away into the clouds, but I was left behind.[r]

I also tried to hide, but I couldn't, because the man who sat on the cloud had his piercing eyes fixed on me. I was also convicted by my own conscience that I was unworthy[s]. Then I thought about crying out to the rocks to cover me, but they would not. Besides, I was ashamed, for all my sins were now public. And then I woke up from my sleep."

"But what was it about this sight that made you so afraid?" Christian asked.

"Well, I thought the day of judgment had come and that I was not ready for it," the man replied. "But the most dreadful part was that I thought the Judge had his eyes on me, and my conscience accused me from every side. And then I woke up, just as you see me."

Then the Interpreter said to Christian, "Have you considered all these things?"

"Yes," said Christian, "and they fill me with both hope and fear."

"Good," said the Interpreter. "Keep all these things in your mind so that they may be like a spur in your side to urge you forward on the path you must travel." Then Christian prepared himself to continue his journey. The Interpreter said, "May the Comforter be with you always, good Christian, to guide you in the way that leads to the City." So, Christian went on his way, saying:

"Here I have seen things rare and of great worth,
Things pleasant, dreadful, to give my faith birth,
And make me stable in the path I take.
Let me reflect on them for my own sake,
Understand why they were shown to me,
And be forever thankful, friend, to thee."

---

[a] *1Co. 4:15*
[b] *Gal. 4:19*
[c] *Rom. 7:6; 1Co. 15:56; Rom. 5:20*
[d] *Jhn. 15:3; Eph. 5:26; Act. 15:9; Rom. 16:25-26; Jhn. 15:13*
[e] *Luk. 16:25*
[f] *2Co. 4:18*
[g] *2Co. 12:9*
[h] *Act. 14:22*
[i] *Luk. 8:13*
[j] *Heb. 6:6*
[k] *Luk. 19:14*
[l] *Heb. 10:28-29*
[m] *1Co. 15:52; 1 Th 4:16; Jud 1:14; Jhn 5:28-29; 2 Th 1:7-8; Rev 20:11-14*
[n] *Isa. 26:21; Mic 7:16-17; Psa 95:1-3; Dan 7:10*
[o] *Mal. 3:2-3; Dan 7:9-10*
[p] *Mat. 3:12; Mat 13:30; Mal 4:1*
[q] *Luk. 3:17*
[r] *1Th. 4:16-17*
[s] *Rom. 3:14-15*

Chapter 5: The Cross and The Hill of Difficulty

Who is this man? The Pilgrim, it is true,
The old has passed, and all things are made new.
He is transformed, a man of different worth,
A change of heart has brought a new birth.

Now I saw in my dream that the highway Christian was to travel was fenced on both sides with a wall, and that wall was called Salvation.[a] Christian ran up this path, but not without great difficulty, because of the load on his back.

He ran this way until he came to a place with a small hill. On that place stood a cross, and below it was a tomb. I saw in my dream that just as Christian came up to the cross, his burden loosened from his shoulders, fell from his back, and began to tumble. It continued to roll until it came to the entrance to the tomb, where it fell in, and I saw it no more.

Then Christian was glad and lighthearted, and he said with a joyful heart, "He has given me rest by His sorrow, and life by His death." He stood still for a while to look and wonder, for it was very surprising to him that the sight of the cross could relieve him of his burden in this way. He looked and looked again, until the tears streamed down his cheeks.[b]

Now, as he stood there looking and weeping, three shining ones came to him and greeted him with, "Peace be with you." The first said to him, "Your sins are forgiven." The second stripped him of his rags and gave him new clothes.[c] The third set a mark on his forehead and gave him a sealed scroll[1], which he was told to look at as he ran and to present at the Celestial Gate.[d] Then they went on their way.

Then Christian gave three leaps for joy and went on his way, singing:

---

[1] *The sealed scroll is a key symbol in the story. It is a common interpretation that it represents the* ***assurance of salvation*** *and the promises of God's Word, which Christian must hold onto and present at the Celestial Gate.*

"Thus far I came, weighed down with all my sin,
And nothing could relieve the grief within
Until I came here. What a place is this!
Is this where all my happiness begins?
Is this where the burden falls from off my back?
Is this where the ropes that bound it to me crack?
Blessed cross! Blessed tomb! But blessed be
The Man who there was put to shame for me!"

I saw then in my dream that he continued on this way until he came to the bottom of the hill, where he saw, a little off the path, three men fast asleep with chains on their heels. The name of the first was **Simple**, the second was **Sloth**, and the third was **Presumption**.

Seeing them in this state, Christian went to them to see if he could wake them. He cried out, "You are like men sleeping at the top of a mast, for the dead sea is under you—a gulf that has no bottom![e] Wake up and come away! If you are willing, I will help you get those chains off." He also told them, "If the one who prowls around like a roaring lion comes by, you will surely fall prey to his claws and teeth.[f]"

Christian discovers Simple, Sloth, and Presumption

They looked at him and began to answer. Simple said, "I see no danger." Sloth said, "Just a little more sleep." And Presumption said, "Every tub must stand on its own bottom." And with that they lay down to sleep again, and Christian went on his way.

Yet he was troubled to think that men in such danger would have so little respect for the kindness of someone who so freely offered to help them by waking them, advising them, and offering to help them remove their chains. And as he was thinking about this, he saw two men come tumbling over the wall on the left side of the narrow way, and they hurried to catch up with him. The name of the first was **Formalist**, and the name of the other was **Hypocrisy**.

"Gentlemen, where did you come from, and where are you going?" Christian asked.

Formalist and Hypocrisy answered, "We were born in the land of **Vain-glory**, and we are going to Mount Zion to seek praise."

"Why didn't you come in through the gate that stands at the beginning of the path?" Christian asked. "Don't you know it is written that anyone who does not enter by the door, 'but climbs in by some other way, is a thief and a robber'?"[g]

They said, "It is not just us; all our countrymen consider going to the gate for entrance to be too far out of the way. Therefore, our usual method is to take a shortcut and climb over the wall, just as we have done."

"But won't it be considered a trespass against the Lord of the city where we are headed, to violate His revealed will like this?" Christian pressed.

They told him that he didn't need to trouble his head about it, because what they did was based on custom. If needed, they could produce proof that people had been doing it this way for more than a thousand years.

"But" Christian asked, "will your practice hold up in the court of judgement?"

They told him that a custom that has been established for over a thousand years would undoubtedly be accepted as legal by any impartial judge. "Besides," they said, "if we get onto the path, what does it matter how we get on it? If we are on it, we are on it. You are on the path, and from what we can tell, you came in through the gate. We are also on the path, and we came by tumbling over the wall. How is your situation any better than ours?"

"I walk by the rule of my Master; you walk by the crude impulses of your own imaginations," Christian replied. "You are already considered thieves by the Lord of this way; therefore, I doubt you will be found to be true men at the end of the journey. You came in by yourselves, without His direction, and you will go out by yourselves, without His mercy."

To this, they gave him little reply, only telling him to mind his own business. Then I saw that they all went on, each in his own way, without much more conversation. The only other thing the two men said to Christian was that, as for laws and regulations, they had no doubt they would obey them just as dutifully as he would. "Therefore," they said, "we see no way in which you are different from us, except for the coat on your back, which we suppose was given to you by some of your neighbors to hide the shame of your nakedness."

"You will not be saved by laws and regulations, since you did not come in through the door,[h]" Christian replied. "As for this coat on my back, it was given to me by the Lord of the place where I am going, and it was, as you say, to cover my nakedness. I take it as a token of His kindness to me, for I had nothing but rags before. Besides, I comfort myself with this thought as I go: 'Surely, when I come to the gate of the city, the Lord there will recognize me, since I have His coat on my back—a coat He gave me freely on the day He stripped me of my rags.' I also have a mark on my forehead, which perhaps you haven't noticed, that one of my Lord's most intimate companions placed there on the day my burden fell from my shoulders. Furthermore, I will tell you that I was given a sealed scroll to comfort me by reading it as I travel. I was also told to present it at the Celestial Gate as assurance that I will certainly be allowed inside. I suspect you lack all these things, and you lack them because you did not come in through the gate."

They gave him no answer to these things but only looked at each other and laughed. Then I saw that they all went on, but Christian kept ahead of them. He had no more conversation with them, but spoke only to himself, sometimes sighing and sometimes taking comfort. When he needed refreshing, he would also often read from the scroll that one of the shining ones had given him.

I saw then that they all went on until they came to the foot of the **Hill of Difficulty**, at the bottom of which was a spring. In that same place, there were two other paths besides the one that came straight from the gate. One turned to the left and the other to the right at the bottom of the hill. But the narrow way went straight up the hill, and the path up the side of the hill was called Difficulty. Christian now went to the spring and drank from it to refresh himself,[i] and then he began to go up the hill, saying:

"The hill, though high, I desire to ascend,
The difficulty will not me offend;
For I can see the way to life lies here.
Come, take heart, let's neither faint nor fear.
Better, though difficult, the right way to go,
Than wrong, though easy, where the end is woe."

The other two also came to the foot of the hill. But when they saw that the hill was steep and high, and that there were two other ways to go, they supposed that these two paths might meet up again with Christian's path on the other side. Therefore, they decided to take those other ways. Now, the name of one of those paths was **Danger**, and the name of the other was **Destruction**. So, the first took the path called Danger, which led him into a great forest, and the other took the path to Destruction, which led him into a wide field full of dark mountains, where he stumbled and fell, and never rose again.

---

[a] *Isa. 26:1*
[b] *Zec. 12:10*
[c] *Zec. 3:4*
[d] *Eph. 1:13*
[e] *Pro. 23:34*
[f] *1Pe. 5:8*
[g] *Jhn. 10:1*
[h] *Gal. 2:16*
[i] *Isa. 49:10*

Chapter 6: The Arbor and the Lions

Shall they who wrong begin yet rightly end?
Shall they at all have safety for their friend?
No, no; in headstrong manner they set out,
And headlong will they fall at last, no doubt.

I looked then to see Christian go up the hill. I noticed he went from running to walking, and from walking to clambering on his hands and knees because the place was so steep. Now, about halfway to the top of the hill was a pleasant arbor, a small shelter made of latticework and covered with vines, built by the Lord of the hill for the refreshment of weary travelers. Christian made his way there and sat down to rest. He pulled his scroll out from his shirt and read from it for his comfort. He also took a moment to look again at the coat that was given to him when he stood by the cross.

As he was enjoying this for a while, he at last fell into a slumber, and from there into a deep sleep, which kept him in that place until it was almost night. And in his sleep, his scroll fell from his hand. Now, as he was sleeping, someone came to him and woke him up, saying, "Go to the ant, you sluggard; consider its ways and be wise.[a]" And with that, Christian jumped up and hurried on his way, walking quickly until he came to the top of the hill.

When he got to the top of the hill, two men came running to meet him at full speed. The name of the first was **Timorous**, and the name of the other was **Mistrust**. Christian said to them, "Sirs, what's the matter? You're running the wrong way." Timorous answered that they had been going to the City of Zion and had made it up that difficult hill. "But," he said, "the farther we go, the more danger we meet. That is why we turned around and are going back again."

"Yes," said Mistrust, "for just ahead of us, there are a couple of lions in the path. We don't know if they're sleeping or awake, but we were sure that if we got within their reach, they would tear us to pieces."

Then Christian said, "You make me afraid, but where can I flee to be safe? If I go back to my own country, it is destined for fire and brimstone, and I will certainly perish there. If I can get to the Celestial City, I am sure to be safe there. I must take the risk. To go back is nothing but death; to go forward is the fear of death, but with everlasting life beyond it. I will keep going forward."

So, Mistrust and Timorous ran down the hill, and Christian went on his way. But thinking again about what he had heard from the men, he felt in his shirt for his scroll so that he might read it and be comforted, but when he felt for it, it was missing!

Then Christian was in great distress. He did not know what to do, for he was missing the very thing that had comforted him during the difficult parts of his journey and the thing that was meant to be his pass into the Celestial City! He began to be very perplexed and did not know what to do. At last, he remembered that he had slept in the resting spot on the side of the hill. Falling to his knees, he asked God for forgiveness for his foolish act and then went back to look for his scroll. But all the way back, who can fully describe the sorrow in Christian's heart? Sometimes he sighed, sometimes he wept, and often he scolded himself for being so foolish as to fall asleep in that place, which was built only for a little refreshment from his weariness.

So, he went back, carefully looking on this side and that all along the way, hoping he might find the scroll that had been his comfort so many times on his journey. He went on like this until he came again within sight of the arbor where he had sat and slept. But that sight only renewed his sorrow more by bringing his sin of sleeping fresh into his mind.[b] So he now went on, mourning his sinful sleep and saying, "Oh, what a wretched man I am! To sleep in the daytime! To sleep in the middle of a great difficulty! To indulge my body by using that rest for physical ease, when the Lord of the hill built it only for the relief of the spirits of pilgrims!"

"How many steps I have taken in vain! This is what happened to Israel for their sin; they were sent back again by way of the Red Sea. And I am forced to walk these steps with sorrow, which I might have walked with delight if it had not been for this sinful sleep. How far along my way I could have been by now! I am forced to walk these steps three times over, when I only needed to walk them once. And yes, now I will likely be caught by the night, for the day is almost over. Oh, if only I had not slept!"

Now by this time, he had come to the resting spot again. There he sat down and wept for a while. But at last, as Providence would have it, he looked sorrowfully down under the bench and saw his scroll. With trembling and haste, he snatched it up and put it in his shirt. Who can describe how joyful this man was when he had his scroll again! For this scroll was the assurance of his life and his acceptance at the desired haven. Therefore, he put it away safely, gave thanks to God for directing his eyes to the place where it lay, and with joy and tears, he set out again on his journey.

Oh, how nimbly he went up the rest of the hill! Yet, before he reached the top, the sun went down on Christian. This made him again remember the foolishness of his sleeping, and he began to berate himself again. "Oh, you sinful sleep," he said, "because of you, I will likely be caught by the night on my journey! I must walk without the sun, darkness will cover my path, and I must hear the noise of dreadful creatures, all because of my sinful sleep.[c]" Now he also remembered the story that Mistrust and Timorous had told him, of how they were frightened by the sight of the lions. Then Christian said to himself again, "These beasts hunt for their prey at night. If they should meet me in the dark, how could I fight them? How could I escape being torn to pieces by them?"

And so, he went on his way. But while he was mourning his unfortunate mistake, he lifted his eyes, and there before him was a very stately palace. Its name was **Beautiful**[1], and it stood right beside the highway.

So, he hurried forward, hoping he might find lodging there. Before he had gone far, he entered a very narrow passage. About a stone's throw ahead, near the main gate of the palace, stood a small gatehouse for the porter, called the **porter's lodge**. Looking very carefully ahead of him as he went, he saw two lions in the path.

---

[1] Most scholars agree that the Palace Beautiful represents the organized church. It serves as an allegory for a place of rest, instruction, fellowship, and encouragement for pilgrims on their journey.

Now, he thought, *I see the dangers that drove Mistrust and Timorous back.* (The lions were chained, but he did not see the chains.) Then he was afraid and thought about turning back to follow them, for he could imagine nothing but death ahead of him.

But the porter at the lodge, whose name was **Watchful**, saw that Christian had stopped as if he were going to turn back. He cried out to him, saying, "Is your strength so small? Do not fear the lions, for they are chained. They are placed here to test the faith of those who have it and to reveal those who have none. Stay in the middle of the path, and no harm will come to you."

---

[a] *Pro. 6:6*
[b] *Rev. 2:5; 1Th. 5:7-8*
[c] *1Th. 5:6-7*

Chapter 7: The Palace Beautiful

The path is hard, and he who stays the course
Must draw upon a strength beyond his force.
Though snares and dangers on each side may lie,
The virtuous man will pass them safely by.

Then I saw that he went forward, trembling in fear of the lions but paying close attention to the porter's directions. He heard the lions roar, but they did him no harm. Then he clapped his hands and continued on until he came and stood before the gate where the porter was.

"Sir, what house is this?" Christian asked the porter. "And may I lodge here tonight?"

The porter answered, "This house was built by the Lord of the hill, and He built it for the relief and security of pilgrims." The porter also asked him where he was from and where he was going.

"I have come from the City of Destruction, and I am going to Mount Zion," Christian said. "But because the sun has now set, I would like to lodge here tonight, if I may."

"What is your name?" the porter asked.

"My name is now Christian, but at first, my name was Graceless," he answered. "I come from the race of Japheth, whom God will persuade to dwell in the tents of Shem.[a]"[1]

"But how did it happen that you have come so late? The sun is set."

"I would have been here sooner, but—wretched man that I am! – I slept in the resting spot that stands on the hillside," Christian explained. "And even so, I would have been here much sooner, but in my sleep, I lost my scroll and arrived at the top of the hill without it. When I felt for

---

[1] *This is a reference to Noah's prophecy in Genesis 9:27. In some Christian traditions, Noah's son Shem was the ancestor of the Israelites, while his brother Japheth was the ancestor of the Gentiles (non-Jews). The prophecy that Japheth would "dwell in the tents of Shem" was seen as a promise that Gentiles would be brought into God's covenant family through faith in Christ. Christian is identifying himself as a Gentile who has become part of the household of faith.*

it and did not find it, I was forced, with a sorrowful heart, to go back to the place where I had slept. I found it there, and now I have finally come."

"Well," the porter said, "I will call one of the maidens of this place. If she likes what you have to say, she will bring you into the rest of the household, according to the rules of the house." So **Watchful**, the porter, rang a bell. At the sound, a serious and beautiful young woman named **Discretion** came to the door and asked why she had been called.

The porter answered, "This man is on a journey from the City of Destruction to Mount Zion and wishes to know if he may lodge here tonight. I have asked his name, and he has told me it is Christian."

"We have lodged a great many pilgrims here lately," the porter added. Then she asked Christian where he was from and where he was going, and he told her. She also asked him how he got onto the path, and he told her. Then she asked him what he had seen and encountered along the way, and he told her. Finally, she asked him his name. He said, "It is Christian, and I have an even greater desire to lodge here tonight because I see this place was built for the relief and security of pilgrims."

She smiled, but tears welled up in her eyes. After a short pause, she said, "I will call two or three more of the family." She ran to the door and called for **Prudence**, **Piety**, and **Charity**. After they had spoken with him for a little while, they welcomed him into the household. Many of them met him at the doorway of the house and said, "Come in, you who are blessed by the Lord. This house was built by the Lord of the hill on purpose to entertain pilgrims like you."

Then he bowed his head and followed them into the house. When he had come in and sat down, they gave him something to drink. They all agreed that while they waited for supper to be ready, some of them should have a private conversation with Christian to make the best use of the time. They appointed Piety, Prudence, and Charity to speak with him, and this is how they began.

"Come, good Christian," Piety began, "since we have been so loving as to receive you into our house tonight, let us talk with you about everything that has happened on your pilgrimage, so that we may learn from your experiences."

"With all my heart," Christian replied. "I am glad that you are so willing."

"What first motivated you to begin a pilgrim's life?" Piety asked.

"I was driven out of my native country by a dreadful sound in my ears," Christian answered. "It was the sound of certain, unavoidable destruction that awaited me if I remained in that place."

"But how did it happen that you came out of your country by this specific path?"

"It was as God willed it," Christian said. "For when I was terrified of destruction, I did not know where to go. But by chance, as I was trembling and weeping, a man named Evangelist came to me. He directed me to the wicket-gate, which I would have never found otherwise, and he set me on the path that has led me directly to this house."

"But did you not come by the house of the Interpreter?" Piety asked.

"Yes, and I saw things there that I will remember as long as I live," Christian said. "Especially three things: how Christ, in spite of Satan, maintains His work of grace in the heart; how the man in the cage had sinned himself completely beyond the hope of God's mercy; and the dream of the man who thought in his sleep that the day of judgment had come."

"You mean you heard him tell his dream?"

"Yes, and it was a dreadful one. I thought my heart would ache as he was telling it, but I am still glad I heard it."

"Was that everything you saw at the Interpreter's house?" Piety asked.

"No," Christian answered. "He took me to a place where he showed me a stately palace and how the people in it were dressed in gold. He showed me how a courageous man came and cut his way through the armed men who stood at the door to keep him out, and how he was invited to come in and win eternal glory. I thought those things would thrill my heart! I would have stayed at that good man's house for a year, but I knew I had farther to go."

"And what else did you see on the way?" Piety asked.

"What did I see?" Christian replied. "Why, I went only a little farther, and I saw someone—as I imagined in my mind—hanging and bleeding on a tree. The very sight of him made my burden fall off my back, for I was groaning under a very heavy burden, but then it just fell off me. It was a strange thing to me, for I had never seen anything like it before. And yes, while I stood looking up—for I could not stop looking—three shining ones came to me. One of them testified that my sins were forgiven. Another stripped me of my rags and gave me this embroidered coat you see. And the third set the mark you see on my forehead and gave me this sealed scroll." And with that, he pulled it out from his shirt.

Then **Prudence** thought it would be good to ask him a few questions.

"Do you ever think about the country you came from?" she asked.

"Yes, but with much shame and disgust," Christian answered. "'If I had been longing for the country I had left, I might have been tempted to return; but now I desire a better country, a heavenly one.[b]'"

"Do you still carry with you some of the things you were familiar with in your former condition?" Prudence asked.

"Yes, but greatly against my will," he admitted. "Especially my internal, worldly thoughts, which all my countrymen, as well as myself, used to enjoy. But now all those things are a source of grief to me. If I could only choose my own thoughts, I would choose to never think of those things again. But when I want to do what is best, what is worst is always with me.[c]"

"And is it now your main goal to think about what you were before you started on this path?" Prudence inquired.

"No, not if I can help it," Christian said. "I would rather have my mind filled with the new joys I have found since I left home."

"What are the new joys you have found?"

"I have been very delighted with the sight of my Lord's coat on my back, with the mark that is on my forehead, and with the sealed scroll that I carry in my shirt."

"And what is it that makes you so eager to go to Mount Zion?" Prudence asked.

"Why, there I hope to see Him alive who hung dead on the cross," Christian answered. "And there I hope to be rid of all those things that are still an annoyance to me. They say there is no death there,[d] and I will live with the company I like best. For, to tell you the truth, I love Him because He relieved me of my burden, and I am weary of my internal sickness. I long to be where I will die no more, and with the company that will continually cry, 'Holy, Holy, Holy.'"

Then **Charity** said to Christian, "Do you have a family? Are you a married man?"

"I have a wife and four small children," Christian replied.

"And why did you not bring them along with you?"

Then Christian wept and said, "Oh, how willingly I would have done it! But all of them were completely opposed to my going on this pilgrimage."

"But you should have talked to them and tried to show them the danger of being left behind," Charity said.

"I did," Christian answered. "I also told them what God had shown me about the destruction of our city, but 'I seemed to them as one who was joking,' and they did not believe me.[e]"

"And did you pray to God to help them understand your warnings?" Charity asked.

"Yes, with all my heart," Christian answered, "for you must know how dearly I love my wife and children."

"But did you also share your own grief and terror with them?" she pressed. "I assume your fear was obvious enough."

"Yes, over and over and over," he said. "They could also see my fears in my expression, in my tears, and in my trembling at the thought of the judgment that hung over our heads. But none of it was enough to persuade them to come with me."

"But what reason could they give for not coming?" Charity asked.

"Well, my wife was afraid of losing this world, and my children were devoted to the foolish delights of youth," Christian explained. "So, between one thing and another, they left me to wander in this manner alone."

"But did your own lifestyle ever undermine your message?" Charity asked. "Did your actions sometimes contradict your words?"

"I certainly cannot boast about my life, for I am well aware of my many failings," Christian admitted. "I know that a person's conduct can easily tear down the very truths they are trying to build up in others. Yet, I can say this: I was incredibly careful not to give them any reason, through my own inappropriate actions, to be turned off from the pilgrimage. In fact, it was the opposite. They would often tell me I was *too* strict, and that I denied myself things they saw no harm in. No, I truly believe that if anything they saw in me hindered them, it was my deep distress over sinning against God or wronging my neighbor."

Charity replied, "Indeed, Cain hated his brother 'because his own works were evil and his brother's righteous.[f]' And if your wife and children were offended with you for this, they show themselves to be hostile to what is good, and 'you have delivered your soul from their blood.[g]'"

Now I saw in my dream that they sat talking together like this until supper was ready. When the meal was prepared, they sat down to eat. The table was furnished "with the finest foods and the best wines," and all their talk at the table was about the Lord of the hill—namely, what He had done, why He did it, and why He had built that house. From what they said, I understood that He had been a great warrior and had fought with and killed "him who holds the power of death,[h]" but not without great danger to Himself, which made me love Him all the more.

"For, as they said, and as I believe," said Christian, "He did it with the loss of much blood. But what put the glory of grace into everything He did was that He did it out of pure love for His people. And besides, some of the household said they had seen and spoken with Him since He died on the cross. They testified that they heard it from His own lips that He is such a lover of poor pilgrims that there is no one like Him from the east to the west."

They also gave an example of what they claimed, which was that He had stripped Himself of His glory so that He could do this for the poor. And they heard Him say and declare "that He would not dwell on the mountain of Zion alone." Furthermore, they said that He had made many pilgrims into princes, though by nature they were born beggars and had come from the dunghill.[i]

They continued their conversation like this until late at night. After they had committed themselves to their Lord for protection, they went to bed. They put the Pilgrim in a large upper bedroom whose window opened toward the sunrise. The name of the room was **Peace**. He slept there until the break of day, and when he awoke, he sang:

"Where am I now? Is this the love and care Of Jesus, for the people who pilgrims are? To so provide! That I should be forgiven, And dwell already at the door of heaven!"

In the morning, they all got up, and after some more conversation, they told him that he could not leave until they had shown him the rare treasures of that place. First, they took him into the study, where they showed him records of the greatest antiquity. As I remember my dream, they first showed him the family tree of the Lord of the hill, showing that He was the Son of the Ancient of Days and came by an eternal generation. Here also were more fully recorded the deeds He had done and the names of many hundreds He had taken into His service, and how He had placed them in homes that could not be destroyed by the passing of time or the decay of nature.

Then they read to him some of the worthy acts that some of His servants had done: how they had "conquered kingdoms, administered justice, and gained what was promised; who shut the mouths of lions, quenched the fury of the flames, and escaped the edge of the sword; whose weakness was turned to strength; and who became powerful in battle and routed foreign armies.[j]"

Then they read again in another part of the house's records, where it showed how willing their Lord was to receive anyone into His favor, even those who in the past had greatly insulted His person and His work. Here also were several other histories of many other famous things, all of which Christian was shown, things both ancient and modern, along with prophecies and predictions of things that would certainly come to pass, both to the dread and amazement of His enemies and to the comfort and encouragement of pilgrims.

---

[a] *Gen. 9:27*
[b] *Heb. 11:15-16*
[c] *Rom. 7:16-19*
[d] *Isa. 25:8; Rev 21:4*
[e] *Gen. 19:14*
[f] *1Jn. 3:12*
[g] *Eze. 3:19*
[h] *Heb. 2:14-15*
[i] *1Sa. 2:8; Psa 113:7*
[j] *Heb. 11:33-34*

Chapter 8: The Armory and the Valley of Humiliation

'Tis difficult for saints to keep their stand,
When face to face with foes they have at hand;
Their courage and their skill will here be tried,
And they will see what armor God provides.

The next day they took him again into the armory, where they showed him all kinds of equipment their Lord had provided for pilgrims: sword, shield, helmet, breastplate, all-prayer, and shoes that would not wear out. And there was enough here to arm as many men for the service of their Lord as there are stars in the sky.

They also showed him some of the instruments with which some of His servants had done wonderful things. They showed him Moses' rod, the hammer and nail with which Jael killed Sisera, and the pitchers, trumpets, and lamps with which Gideon put the armies of Midian to flight. Then they showed him the ox goad, a long prodding stick, with which Shamgar killed six hundred men. They also showed him the jawbone with which Samson performed such mighty feats. They showed him, moreover, the sling and stone with which David killed Goliath of Gath, and the sword with which their Lord will kill the Man of Sin on the day He rises up to claim His prey. They showed him many other excellent things besides, with which Christian was greatly delighted. After this was done, they went to bed again.

Then I saw in my dream that the next morning he got up to go forward, but they asked him to stay until the next day. "And then," they said, "if the day is clear, we will show you the **Delectable Mountains**, which will add even more to your comfort, because they are nearer to your desired haven." So he agreed and stayed.

When the morning came, they took him to the top of the house and told him to look south. He did, and in the far distance, he saw a most pleasant, mountainous country, beautiful with woods, vineyards, all sorts of fruits, and flowers, with springs and fountains that were a delight to see.[a] Then he asked the name of the country. They said it was **Immanuel's Land**. "And it is for all pilgrims, just as this hill is," they said. "When you get there, you will be able to see the gate of the Celestial City, as the shepherds who live there will show you."

Christian thought it was now time to continue on his journey, and his hosts agreed. "But first," they said, "let us go again into the armory." So, they did, and when he came there, they armed him from head to foot with armor that had been tested, in case he should meet with attacks on the way. Being armed in this way, he walked out with his friends to the gate. There he asked the porter if he had seen any other pilgrims pass by. The porter answered, "Yes."

"Pray, did you know him?" Christian asked.

"I asked his name, and he told me it was Faithful," the porter replied.

"Oh," said Christian, "I know him! He is my townsman, my near neighbor. He comes from the place where I was born. How far ahead do you think he is?"

"By this time, he has gotten below the hill."

"Well, good porter," said Christian, "the Lord be with you, and may He add greatly to all your blessings for the kindness you have shown me."

He began to set out on his own, but Discretion, Piety, Charity, and Prudence insisted on accompanying him down to the foot of the hill. So, they went on together, repeating their earlier conversations, until they came to the descent. Then Christian said, "Just as it was difficult coming up, from what I can see, it is dangerous going down."

"Yes, it is," said Prudence, "for it is a hard thing for a man to go down into the **Valley of Humiliation**, as you are now, and not to slip along the way. That is why we have come out to accompany you down the hill." So, he began to go down, but very cautiously, yet he still slipped once or twice.

Then I saw in my dream that when Christian had gone to the bottom of the hill, these good companions gave him a loaf of bread, a bottle of wine, and a cluster of raisins. And then he went on his way.

---

[a] *Isa. 33:16-17*

Chapter 9: The Battle with Apollyon

The soul of man is pulled by diverse sects,
By good and bad, as this world's scene directs:
Christ pulls, the Devil pulls, and all about
The world and flesh, until the man cries out.

But now, in this **Valley of Humiliation**, poor Christian was under great strain. He had gone only a little way when he caught sight of a foul fiend coming across the field to meet him. His name was **Apollyon**.[1] Fear immediately gripped Christian, and he wrestled with the choice: should he go back, or stand his ground? But then a dreadful realization stopped him: his back was completely unarmored. He knew that to turn and flee would only make him an easy target for the fiend's arrows. Caught between two fears, he understood that his best chance for survival was to stand his ground and fight.

Apollyon confronted him in the midst of the valley. The monster was hideous to behold. He was covered with scales like a fish (which were his pride), he had wings like a dragon, feet like a bear, and out of his belly came fire and smoke. His mouth was like the mouth of a lion. When he came up to Christian, he looked at him with a scornful expression and began to question him.

"Where have you come from," Apollyon demanded, "and where are you going?"

"I have come from the City of Destruction, which is the place of all evil, and I am going to the City of Zion," Christian answered.

"Ah, so you are one of my subjects," Apollyon said, "for all that country is mine, and I am the prince and god of it. How is it that you have run away from your king?" he asked. "If I did not think you might

---

[1] Apollyon is the Greek name used in the book of Revelation for the Hebrew "Abaddon," meaning "The Destroyer." In Revelation 9:11, he is named as the angel-prince of the bottomless pit. Bunyan uses this name to personify the terrifying, destructive, and direct satanic opposition that a pilgrim may face.

still be useful to me, I would strike you down to the ground with one blow."

"It is true I was born in your dominion," Christian replied, "but your service was hard, and no man can survive with your wages, 'for the wages of sin is death.'[a] Therefore, when I came of age, I did what any thinking person would do: I looked for a way to better myself."

"There is no prince who will so lightly lose his subjects, and I will not lose you either," Apollyon roared. "But since you complain about my service and wages, just be content to go back. I promise to give you all our country has to offer."

"But I have pledged my service to another, to the King of Princes himself," said Christian. "How can I possibly go back with you now?"

"You have, according to the proverb, 'exchanged a bad for a worse,'" Apollyon replied. "But it is common for those who claim to be His servants to give Him the slip after a while and return to me. You should do the same, and all will be well."

"I have given Him my faith and sworn my allegiance to Him," Christian declared. "How, then, can I go back on this and not be hanged as a traitor?"

"You did the same for me," Apollyon said, "and yet I am willing to overlook everything if you will just turn around and come back now."

"What I promised you, I promised in my youth and ignorance," Christian answered. "Besides, the Prince under whose banner I now stand has released me from that promise and also pardoned me for collaborating with you in the past. And to tell the truth, destroying Apollyon, I like His service, His wages, His servants, His government, His companions, and His country better than yours. So, stop trying to persuade me! I am His servant, and I will follow Him."

"Think again, when you have a clear head, about what you are likely to face on the path you are taking," Apollyon warned. "You know that most of His servants come to a bad end because they are rebels against me and my ways. How many of them have been put to shameful deaths! And besides, you consider His service better than mine, yet He has never come down to deliver even one of His servants from their enemies. But as for me, the world knows all too well the many times I have delivered—either by power or by trickery—those who have faithfully served me from

Him and His followers, even after they were captured. I will deliver you in the same way."

"He allows their love to be tested, to see whether they will hold fast to Him to the end," Christian replied. "And as for immediate deliverance, they do not seek it or expect it. They are waiting for their glory. And they will have it when their Prince comes in His own glory and in the glory of the angels."

Apollyon sneered, "You have already been unfaithful in your service to him. How do you expect to receive wages from him?"

"When have I been unfaithful to Him, Apollyon?" Christian asked.

"You stumbled at the very start of your journey, when you nearly choked in the Slough of Despond," Apollyon accused. "You sought shortcuts to release your burden, when you should have waited for your Prince to take it off. You sinfully slept and lost your scroll. You were almost persuaded to turn back at the sight of the lions. And when you talk of your journey and of what you have heard and seen, you are filled with an inward desire for personal glory in all that you say and do."

"All this is true," Christian replied, "and much more besides! But the Prince whom I serve and honor is merciful and ready to forgive. Besides, these weaknesses took hold of me in your country. It was there that I absorbed them. I have groaned under them, been sorry for them, and I have obtained the pardon of my Prince."

Then Apollyon burst into a furious rage, saying, "I am an enemy to this Prince! I hate His person, His laws, and His people! I have come to destroy you!"

"Apollyon, beware what you do," Christian commanded, "for I am on the King's highway, the way of holiness. Therefore, take heed."

Then Apollyon straddled the entire width of the path and said, "I have no fear in this matter. Prepare yourself to die, for I swear by my infernal den that you shall go no farther. Here I will spill your soul."

And with that, he threw a flaming arrow at Christian's chest. But Christian deflected the arrow with his shield.

Christian leapt into action and drew his sword. Apollyon attacked him with furious strokes, throwing arrows as thick as hail. Despite doing all he could to avoid them, Apollyon wounded him, with arrows striking his head, his hand, and his foot. Christian recoiled from his injuries and

Apollyon pressed his attack even harder. Again, Christian found renewed courage and resisted as bravely as he could.

The terrible combat lasted for more than half a day, until Christian was almost completely spent. Christian's wounds were making him weaker and weaker.

Then Apollyon, seeing his opportunity, began to close in on Christian. Wrestling with him, he flung Christian to the ground and Christian's sword flew from his hand. Then Apollyon said, "I have you now." And with that, he pressed down on him so hard that he almost crushed him to death, and Christian began to despair that his life was ending.

But as God would have it, while Apollyon was preparing to deliver the final blow and put an end to this good man, Christian stretched out his hand for his sword and caught it, saying, "'Rejoice not over me, my enemy! Though I have fallen, I will rise.[b]'" Christian lunged forward and gave him a deadly thrust, which made him recoil as one who had received a mortal wound.

Christian, seeing this, attacked again, saying, "'No, in all these things we are more than conquerors through him who loved us.[c]'" And with that, Apollyon spread his dragon wings and sped away, and Christian, for a season, saw him no more.[d]

No one can imagine, unless they had seen and heard it as I did, what hideous screeching and roaring Apollyon made during the entire fight—he spoke like a dragon. And on the other side, what agonized sighs and groans burst from Christian's heart. His fierce and determined look never wavered until he realized he had wounded Apollyon with his two-edged sword. Then, indeed, he smiled and look upward! But it was the most dreadful fight I have ever seen.

So, when the battle was over, Christian said, "Here I will give thanks to Him who delivered me from the mouth of the lion, to Him who helped me against Apollyon." And so he did, saying:

"Great Beelzebub, the captain of this fiend,
Plotted my ruin, so he sent his friend,
All armed for war; who with a mighty rage
Opposed my path and tried my soul to cage.
He wounded me—my hands, my head, my feet;
No one could see a more unequal meet.
But Jesus my Lord did stand by me,
And did with shield and sword my life set free."

Then a hand came to him with some of the leaves from the tree of life. Christian took them and applied them to the wounds he had received in the battle, and he was healed immediately. He also sat down in that place to eat the bread and drink from the bottle that were given to him at the Palace Beautiful. So, being refreshed, he prepared for his journey, with his sword drawn in his hand, for he said, "I do not know if some other enemy may be nearby." But he met with no other attack from Apollyon throughout the rest of that valley.

---

a Rom. 6:23
b Mic. 7:8
c Rom. 8:37
d Jam. 4:7

Chapter 10: The Valley of the Shadow of Death

Poor man! where art thou now? thy day is night.
Good man, be not cast down, thou yet art right,
Thy way to heaven lies by the gates of hell;
Cheer up, hold out, with thee it shall go well.

Now at the end of this valley was another, called the **Valley of the Shadow of Death**, and the way to the Celestial City lay right through the middle of it. This valley is a very desolate place. The prophet Jeremiah describes it this way: "a wilderness, a land of deserts and of pits, a land of drought and of deep darkness, a land that no one travels through and where no one lives.[a]"

Now here, Christian found himself in a worse situation than in his fight with Apollyon, as you will see from what follows.

I saw then in my dream that when Christian got to the borders of the Shadow of Death, two men met him. They were descendants of the spies who brought back a bad report of the good land,[b] and they were hurrying to go back. Christian spoke to them:

"Where are you going?"

"Back! Back!" they said. "And we would have you do the same, if you value your life or your peace at all."

"Why, what's the matter?" Christian asked.

"Matter!" they exclaimed. "We were going the same way you are, and we went as far as we dared. Indeed, we almost couldn't get back. If we had gone a little farther, we wouldn't be here to bring the news to you."

"But what did you encounter?" Christian asked.

"Why, we were almost in the Valley of the Shadow of Death," they answered. "But by good fortune, we looked ahead and saw the danger before we reached it.[c]"

"But what did you see?" Christian asked.

"What did we see!" the men exclaimed. "Why, the valley itself is as dark as pitch! We also saw hobgoblins, satyrs, and dragons of the pit there. We also heard in that valley a continuous howling and screeching, like a people in unspeakable misery, who were trapped there bound in affliction and chains. And over that valley hang the discouraging clouds of confusion. Death also spreads its wings over it always. In short, it is utterly dreadful and completely without order.[d]"

Then Christian said, "From what you have said, I still believe that this is my way to the desired haven.[e]"

"Let it be your way, then," they replied. "We will not choose it for ours." So, they parted, and Christian went on his way, but he kept his sword drawn in his hand for fear that he might be attacked.

I saw then in my dream that for the entire length of the valley, there was a very deep ditch on the right side. That is the ditch into which the blind have led the blind for all of history, and where they have both miserably perished.[f] On the left side, there was a very dangerous swamp. If even a good man falls into it, he can find no bottom for his foot to stand on. King David once fell into that swamp and would have undoubtedly suffocated in it if He who is able had not pulled him out.[1]

The pathway here was also extremely narrow, which made it even more difficult for good Christian. For when he tried, in the dark, to avoid the ditch on one side, he was in danger of tipping over into the swamp on the other. And when he tried to escape the quagmire, without great care, he was in danger of falling into the ditch. He went on like this, and I heard him sigh bitterly, for besides the dangers mentioned above, the pathway here was so dark that often, when he lifted his foot to step forward, he did not know where or on what it would land.

About the middle of this valley, I saw that the mouth of Hell was there, standing right beside the path. *Now,* thought Christian, *what will I do?* Every so often, the flames and smoke would pour out in such abundance, with sparks and hideous noises (things that had no regard for

---

[1] *The two hazards on either side of the narrow path represent two opposing spiritual errors. It is a common interpretation that the ditch on one side is the error of blind legalism and rigid tradition, while the swamp on the other represents the error of sinking into the despair of sin without hope. The pilgrim's path requires a careful balance between these two dangers.*

Christian's sword, as Apollyon had), that he was forced to put away his sword and take up another weapon, called **All-prayer**.[g] I heard him cry out, "O Lord, I beg you, deliver my soul![h]"

He went on like this for a long time, and still the flames would reach for him. He also heard sorrowful voices and the sound of creatures rushing back and forth, so that sometimes he thought he would be torn to pieces or trampled like mud in the streets.

He saw this frightful sight and heard these dreadful noises for several miles. When he came to a place where he thought he heard a group of fiends coming forward to meet him, he stopped and began to consider what he should do. For a moment, he had half a mind to go back. Then again, he thought he might be halfway through the valley. He also remembered how he had already conquered many dangers, and that the danger of going back might be much greater than going forward. So he resolved to go on.

Yet the fiends seemed to come nearer and nearer. When they had come almost right up to him, he cried out with a powerful voice, "I will walk in the strength of the Lord God!" At that, they fell back and came no closer.

One thing I must not forget to mention: I noticed that poor Christian was now so confused that he did not recognize his own voice. And this is how I realized it: Just when he had come up alongside the mouth of the burning pit, one of the wicked ones got behind him, crept up softly, and whisperingly suggested many terrible blasphemies to him, which he truly thought had come from his own mind. This troubled Christian more than anything he had encountered before—to think that he would now blaspheme the one he had loved so much. Yet, if he could have helped it, he would not have done it. But he did not have the presence of mind either to stop his ears or to recognize where those blasphemies were coming from.

After Christian had traveled in this miserable condition for some time, he thought he heard the voice of a man walking ahead of him, saying, "'Even though I walk through the valley of the shadow of death, I will fear no evil, for you are with me.[i]'"

Then he was glad, and for these reasons:

First, because he gathered from this that someone else who feared God was in this valley, just as he was.

Second, because he understood that God was with them, even in that dark and dismal state.[j] *And why not with me?* he thought, *even if I cannot feel His presence because of the hindrances of this place.*

Third, because he hoped that if he could catch up to them, he would soon have company. So, he went on and called out to the one who was ahead, but the person did not know how to answer, for he also thought he was alone. And soon the day broke. Then Christian said, "He has turned the shadow of death into the morning.[k]"

Now that morning had come, he looked back—not because he wanted to return, but to see by the light of day what hazards he had passed through in the dark. He saw more clearly the ditch on one side and the quagmire on the other, and also how narrow the path was between them. Now he also saw the hobgoblins, satyrs, and dragons of the pit, but they were all far away, for after daybreak they did not come near. Yet they were revealed to him, according to what is written: "He reveals deep things out of darkness and brings deep darkness to light.[l]"

Christian was deeply moved by this deliverance from all the dangers of his lonely path. Though he had feared them more before, he saw them more clearly now because the daylight made them visible. Around this time the sun was rising, and this was another mercy for Christian. For you must note that although the first part of the Valley of the Shadow of Death was dangerous, this second part, which he still had to travel, was even more dangerous.

From the place where he now stood all the way to the end of the valley, the path was full of snares, traps, and nets on one side, and pits, pitfalls, and deep holes on the other. If it had been dark, as it was when he traveled the first part of the way, even if he had a thousand souls, they all would have surely been lost. But as I said, the sun was just now rising. Then he said, "His lamp shone upon my head, and by his light I walked through darkness.[m]"

In this light, therefore, he came to the end of the valley. Now I saw in my dream that at the end of this valley lay blood, bones, ashes, and the mangled bodies of people, even of pilgrims who had gone this way before.

And while I was wondering about the reason for this, I saw a little way ahead of me a cave where giants called **Pagans** had lived.[2] By their power and tyranny, the people whose bones, blood, and ashes lay there had been cruelly put to death.

But Christian went by this place without much danger, which surprised me somewhat. I have learned since, however, that though they are still alive, they have grown so feeble and stiff in their joints—because of old age and the many sharp encounters they had in their younger days—that they can now do little more than sit at the mouth of this cave, grinning at pilgrims as they go by and biting their nails because they cannot get to them.

---

[a] *Jer. 2:6*
[b] *Num. 13*
[c] *Psa. 44:19; Psa. 107:10*
[d] *Job. 3:5; Job. 10:22*
[e] *Jer. 2:6*
[f] *Psa. 69:14-15*
[g] *Eph. 6:18*
[h] *Psa. 116:4*
[i] *Psa. 23:4*
[j] *Job. 9:11*
[k] *Amo. 5:8*
[l] *Job. 12:22*
[m] *Job. 29:3*

---

[2] *In the original 17th-century text, Bunyan names the two giants in this cave "Pope and Pagan." This reflected the common Puritan view of the time, which saw both ancient paganism and the Papacy as tyrannical powers that had persecuted true Christians. To retain the allegorical point about the decline of old spiritual tyrannies without retaining the specific anti-Catholic sentiment of the era, we have taken the editorial liberty of referring to the giants collectively as "Pagans."*

Chapter 11: Christian and Faithful

Here Christian meets a friend, whose latter end
Will be to prove a true and faithful friend,
Who tells him of the trials on the way,
And of his own great struggle in the fray.

Now I saw in my dream that Christian did not go on alone, for there was one whose name was **Faithful**. When Faithful saw Christian, he not only guessed that they were from the same country but also that they were neighbors. Therefore, hearing that Christian was on his journey, he also set out to go with him.

As Christian went on his way, he came to a small hill that had been raised up on purpose so that pilgrims could see what was ahead of them. Christian went up there, and looking forward, he saw Faithful on the path ahead of him. Then Christian called out loudly, "Ho! Ho! Hey! Wait, and I will be your companion!"

At that, Faithful looked behind him. Christian cried out again, "Wait, wait until I catch up to you!"

But Faithful answered, "No, I am running for my life, and the avenger of blood is behind me![a]"

Christian was spurred on by this, and using all his strength, he quickly caught up with Faithful and then ran past him, so the last became first. Then Christian smiled with foolish pride because he had gotten ahead of his brother. But not paying attention to his feet, he suddenly stumbled and fell, and he could not get up again until Faithful came to help him.

Then I saw in my dream that they went on together in a very loving way and had an intimate conversation about all the things that had happened to them on their pilgrimage. This is how Christian began.

"Beloved Faithful," Christian began, "I am glad that I have caught up with you, and that God has enabled us to walk as companions on this very pleasant path."

"I had hoped, friend, that we would be traveling together by now," Faithful replied, "but you got a head start on me, so I was forced to come all this way alone."

"How long did you stay in the City of Destruction before you set out after me on your pilgrimage?" Christian asked.

"Until I could stay no longer," Faithful said. "For soon after you left, there was a great rumor that our city would shortly be burned to the ground with fire from heaven."

"What! And did your neighbors believe the rumor?" Christian asked.

"Yes, I think they did, for they stood staring at me," Faithful said. "But my spirit would not let me stay. I did, however, linger around my own house for a while, hoping I could bring my wife and children with me, but I could not persuade them. So I came on my way."

"But what did your neighbors say to you when they saw you leaving?"

"They called after me, 'Fool! Fool!' and told me I should go back to be saved from the coming fire. But I put my fingers in my ears and came on my way."

"Did you face any assaults as you came?" Christian asked.

"Yes, I met a woman named **Wanton**, who almost did me great harm," Faithful replied.

"It was good that you escaped her net. Joseph was severely tempted by her, and he escaped her as you did, but it almost cost him his life.[b] But what did she do to you?"

"You cannot imagine—unless you know something of her—what a flattering tongue she had," Faithful said. "She pleaded with me to turn aside with her, promising me all kinds of satisfaction."

"No, she did not promise you the satisfaction of a good conscience," Christian observed.

"You know what I mean," said Faithful. "All worldly and fleshly satisfaction."

"Thank God you escaped her," Christian said. "'He who is cursed by the LORD will fall into her pit.'"[c]

"Well, I don't know if I escaped her completely or not."

"Why? Surely you did not consent to her desires?" Christian asked.

"No, not to the point of defiling myself," Faithful answered. "For I remembered an old writing I had seen which said, 'Her steps lead straight to the grave.'[d] So I shut my eyes because I did not want to be bewitched by her looks.[e] Then she cursed at me, and I went on my way."

"Did you face any other assaults as you came?" Christian asked.

"When I came to the foot of the Hill of Difficulty, I met a very old man who asked me who I was and where I was headed," Faithful said. "I told him that I am a pilgrim going to the Celestial City. Then the old man said, 'You look like an honest fellow. Would you be content to live with me for the wages I will give you?' Then I asked him his name and where he lived. He said his name was **Adam the First**,[1] and that he lived in the town of **Deceit**.[f] I then asked him what his work was, and what wages he would give. He told me that his work was full of many delights, and his wages were that I would be his heir in the end. I further asked him what kind of house he kept and what other servants he had. He told me that his house was supplied with all the delicacies in the world and that his servants were his own offspring. Then I asked if he had any children. He said he had only three daughters: the **Lust of the Flesh**, the **Lust of the Eyes**, and the **Pride of Life**,[g] and that I could marry them if I wanted. Then I asked how long he would want me to live with him, and he told me, 'As long as I myself live.'"

"Well, and what was the final outcome between you and the old man?" Christian asked.

"Why, at first, I found myself somewhat inclined to go with the man, for I thought he spoke very reasonably," Faithful said. "But as I was talking with him, I looked at his forehead and saw written there, 'Put off your old self, which belongs to your former manner of life.[h]'"

"And what happened then?"

"Then it came burning hot into my mind that whatever he said and however he flattered, once he got me to his house, he would sell me as a slave. So, I told him to stop talking, for I would not come near the door

---

[1] *It is a common interpretation that Adam the First represents the sinful, unregenerate human nature (the "old man" in Pauline theology) that tempts believers with worldly promises of pleasure and inheritance.*

of his house. Then he cursed me and told me that he would send someone after me who would make my journey bitter to my soul. So, I turned to go away from him. But just as I turned to leave, I felt him grab hold of my flesh and give me such a deadly pull backward that I thought he had torn part of me away with him. This made me cry, 'O wretched man!'[i] And so I went on my way up the hill."

Christian and Faithful

"Now, when I had gotten about halfway up the hill, I looked behind me and saw someone coming after me, as swift as the wind. He overtook me just about the place where the arbor stands."

"Right there," said Christian, "is where I sat down to sleep, and overcome by sleep, I lost this scroll from my shirt."

"But, good brother, let me finish," Faithful said. "As soon as the man overtook me, it was nothing but a word and a blow, for he knocked me down and left me for dead. When I came to my senses again, I asked him why he treated me that way. He said it was because of my secret inclination to go with Adam the First. With that, he struck me another deadly blow on the chest and beat me backward to the ground, so I lay at his feet as dead as before. When I came to myself again, I cried out for mercy, but he said, 'I do not know how to show mercy,' and with that, he knocked me down again. He would have undoubtedly made an end of me, but someone came by and told him to stop."

"Who was it that told him to stop?" Christian asked.

"I didn't recognize him at first," Faithful said, "but as he went by, I saw the holes in his hands and in his side. Then I concluded that he was our Lord. And so, I continued up the hill."

"That man who overtook you was **Moses**,"[2] Christian explained. "He spares no one, nor does he know how to show mercy to those who break his law."

"I know it very well," said Faithful. "It was not the first time he has met me. It was he who came to me when I was living securely at home and told me he would burn my house down over my head if I stayed there."

"But did you not see the house that stood there on the top of the hill, the one where the lions lay by the side of the path?"

"I saw the lions, and I saw the house, but I did not go in," Faithful said. "I was afraid of the lions, and also because it was getting late, so I came on down the hill."

---

[a] *Num. 35:11-12*
[b] *Gen. 39:11-13*
[c] *Psa. 22:14*
[d] *Pro. 5:5*
[e] *Job. 31:1*
[f] *Eph. 4:22*
[g] *1Jn. 2:16*
[h] *Col. 3:9*
[i] *Rom. 7:24*

---

[2] *Here Moses represents the Law of God which he delivered (i.e., the Ten Commandments). From this theological perspective, the Law is perfect and unyielding. It can reveal sin and punish the sinner, but it has no power to show mercy or save. Only Christ can save the pilgrim from the just condemnation of the Law.*

Chapter 12: The Pilgrims Meet Talkative

Here Faithful and his brother Christian meet
A man whose talk is pleasing, soft, and sweet;
But he's a tainted soul, and rotten at the core,
Whose words are for the wind, and nothing more.

Now I saw in my dream that Christian and Faithful went on together, having an intimate conversation about all the things they had seen on their journey. They soon met a man whose name was **Talkative**, and they had a great deal of conversation with him. This Talkative was a tall man and looked a bit more handsome from a distance than he did up close. Faithful addressed him in this way.

"Friend, where are you headed?" Faithful asked. "Are you going to the heavenly country?"

"I am going to that very place," Talkative replied.

"That is good. Then I hope we may have your company."

"I would be very happy to be your companion," said Talkative.

"Come on, then, and let us go together," Faithful said, "and let us spend our time discussing things that are beneficial."

"To talk of good things is very agreeable to me, whether with you or with anyone else," Talkative replied. "And I am glad that I have met people who are so inclined toward such a good work. For, to tell you the truth, there are few who care to spend their time this way while they travel but instead choose to speak of things that are of no benefit, and this has been a great trouble to me."

"That is indeed something to be sad about," Faithful said. "For what things are more worthy of being discussed by men on earth than the things of the God of heaven?"

"I like you very much," Talkative declared, "for what you say is full of conviction. And I will add, what is so pleasant and what is so beneficial as talking about the things of God? What could be more pleasant, that is, if a person has any delight in wonderful things? For instance, if a man loves to talk of the history or the mystery of things, or if a man loves to talk of miracles, wonders, and signs, where will he find things so delightful and so beautifully written as in the Holy Scripture?"

"That's true," said Faithful, "but our goal in such talk should be to truly benefit from these things."

"That is exactly what I said," Talkative replied. "For to talk of such things is most beneficial. By doing so, a person can get to know many things, like the emptiness of earthly things and the value of things above. In this way, a person may learn what it is to repent, to believe, to pray, to suffer, and so on. By this, a person may also learn about the great promises and comforts of the gospel, for his own comfort. Furthermore, by this, a person may learn to refute false opinions, to defend the truth, and also to instruct the ignorant."

"All this is true," said Faithful, "and I am glad to hear these things from you."

"Alas, the lack of this kind of talk is the reason that so few understand the need for faith and the necessity of a work of grace in their soul in order to have eternal life," Talkative continued. "Instead, they ignorantly live by the works of the law, by which no one can ever obtain the kingdom of heaven."

"But, if I may say so," Faithful added, "heavenly knowledge of these things is a gift from God. No one attains it by human effort or simply by talking about them."

"I know all of this very well," Talkative said. "For a man can receive nothing unless it is given to him from heaven; everything is by grace, not by works. I could give you a hundred scriptures to confirm this."

"Well, then," said Faithful, "what is the one thing we should base our conversation on at this time?[a]"

"Whatever you wish," Talkative replied grandly. "I will talk about things heavenly or things earthly; things moral or things of the gospel; things sacred or things secular; things past or things to come; things foreign or things domestic; things essential or things circumstantial, as long as it is all done for our benefit."

Now Faithful began to be amazed. Stepping over to Christian (who had been walking by himself this whole time), he said to him softly, "What a fine companion we have found! Surely this man will make a very excellent pilgrim."

At this, Christian smiled modestly and said, "This man you're so impressed with could fool twenty people who don't know him with that tongue of his."

"You know him, then?" Faithful asked.

"Know him? Yes, better than he knows himself."

"Please, what is he like?"

"His name is Talkative, and he lives in our town," Christian explained. "I'm surprised you have never met him, but then again, I suppose our town is large."

"Whose son is he?" Faithful asked. "And where exactly does he live?"

"He is the son of a man named Say-well, and he lives on Prattling Row," Christian said. "Everyone on Prattling Row knows him simply as Talkative. And despite his fine-sounding tongue, he is a worthless fellow."

"Well, he seems to be a very pleasant man," Faithful remarked.

"That is, to those who don't know him well," Christian replied, "for he is at his best when he is away from home. Up close, he is ugly enough. When you say that he is a 'pleasant man,' it reminds me of something I've observed in the work of a painter, whose pictures look best from a distance but are much less pleasing up close."

"I am glad you have given me this warning," Faithful said. "Let us act wisely now. To do that, I will observe him a little longer and see if I can get him to discuss the power of religion."

"That is a good idea," Christian said, "but be sure you give him a fair opportunity, and then you will see that he will fall silent."

"You speak the truth," Faithful replied, "for his name is Talkative. He is a great talker but a poor doer."

"He is the very stain, reproach, and shame of religion to all who know him," Christian said. "He gives religion a bad name. He is a saint when he is away from home, and a devil when he is at home. His house is as empty of religion as the white of an egg is of flavor. There is no prayer there, nor any sign of repentance for sin. Indeed, even a brute beast serves

God better than he does. He is the very stain, reproach, and shame of religion to all who know him."

"Well, I am sorry to hear such a bad report about him," Faithful said, "but I am sure you are telling the truth, for everyone who knows him has said the same thing."

Talkative Meets the Pilgrims

"For my part, I am not sorry," Christian replied, "for I have gained something from it."

"How so?"

"Why, I have been convinced that it is not enough to talk about religion unless I also live according to what I claim to believe."

"Well, a man may be a hearer of the Word and yet not a doer of it," Faithful said.

"Yes, yes, that is most true," Christian agreed, "and there are many men of that sort. As the apostle says, '...it is not those who hear the law who are righteous in God's sight, but it is those who obey the law who will be declared righteous.[b]'"

"You speak the truth," Faithful said. "Please, what is the difference between talking and doing?"

"A great difference," Christian answered. "A man can talk about a mountain without being able to move it."

"Please, let me hear your thoughts on this matter."

"Well, a man can be a great talker about religion and yet be a complete stranger to its power," Christian explained. "He can have a tongue that speaks of the necessity of a work of grace in the soul, yet his own heart can be a stranger to that work. He may talk about the nature of repentance, faith, hope, and love, yet know nothing of them in his own soul. He may talk of the joys of heaven and yet be a stranger to them.

Yes, a man can have all this and much more and still be nothing but a resounding gong or a clanging cymbal."

"Now I see that saying and doing are two different things," said Faithful, "and from now on I will be more careful to observe the difference."

"They are indeed two different things, and they are as distinct as the soul and the body," Christian said. "For just as the body without the soul is a dead carcass, so also is speaking about God if it does not come with action. The soul of religion is the practical part. 'Religion that God our Father accepts as pure and faultless is this: to look after orphans and widows in their distress and to keep oneself from being polluted by the world.[c]' Talkative is unaware of this principle. He thinks that hearing and saying will make a good Christian, and in this way, he deceives his own soul. Hearing is only the sowing of the seed; talking is not enough to prove that fruit is actually in the heart and life. And let us be assured that on the day of judgment, people will be judged according to their fruit.[d] It will not be asked then, 'Did you believe?' but, 'Were you a doer, or only a talker?' And they will be judged accordingly. The end of the world is compared to a harvest, and you know that at harvest time, people care about nothing but the fruit. Not that anything can be accepted that does not come from faith, but I say this to show you how meaningless Talkative's profession will be on that day."

"Well, I was not so fond of his company at first, but now I am sick of it," Faithful said. "What should we do to get rid of him?"

"Take my advice and do as I tell you," Christian said, "and you will find that he will soon be sick of your company too, unless God touches his heart and turns it."

"What would you have me do?"

"Why, go to him and begin a serious conversation about the power of religion," Christian advised. "And ask him plainly—after he has agreed with the general idea, for he certainly will—whether this power is present in his own heart, his home, or his lifestyle."

Then Faithful stepped forward again and said to Talkative, "Come, what's new? How are things now?"

"Thank you, I am well," Talkative replied. "I thought we would have had a great deal of conversation by this time."

"Well, if you're willing, we can get to it now," said Faithful. "And since you left it to me to choose the question, let it be this: How does the saving grace of God reveal itself when it is in a person's heart?"

"I see, then, that our conversation must be about the power of things," Talkative said. "Well, it is a very good question, and I will be happy to answer you. And here is my answer in brief: First, where the grace of God is in the heart, it causes a great outcry against sin. Second..."

"No, wait," Faithful interrupted. "Let us consider one point at a time. I think you should say, rather, that it shows itself by leading the soul to hate its sin."

"Why, what is the difference between crying out against sin and hating it?" Talkative asked.

"Oh, a great deal," Faithful said. "A man may cry out against sin for strategic reasons, but he cannot truly hate it unless God has transformed his heart to naturally despise it. I have heard many cry out against sin in the pulpit who still tolerate it well enough in their own heart, home, and lifestyle. Joseph's mistress cried out with a loud voice as if she were very holy, but despite that, she would have willingly committed adultery with him. Some people cry out against sin the same way a mother scolds the child on her lap, calling it a naughty little thing, and then immediately starts hugging and kissing it."

"I see you're trying to trap me with my own words," Talkative accused.

"No, not at all," Faithful replied. "I am only trying to set things right. But, let's move on. What is the second sign which would demonstrate a work of grace has transformed someone's heart?"

"A great knowledge of gospel mysteries," Talkative answered.

"This sign should have come first, but whether first or last, it is also false," Faithful said. "For a person can obtain great knowledge in the mysteries of the gospel and yet have no work of grace in his soul. Indeed, even if a man has all knowledge, he may still be nothing, and therefore not be a child of God.

Remember, when Christ asked, 'Do you understand all these things?' and the disciples answered, 'Yes,' He added, 'Blessed are you if you do them.' He does not place the blessing in the knowing of them, but in the doing of them.

We see many examples of people whose knowledge does not lead to actions. They are like the one who 'knows his master's will and does not do it.' A person may be as learned as an angel and yet not be a Christian! Therefore, I must disagree with you. Knowing is what pleases talkers and boasters, but doing is what pleases God.

"That is not to say that the heart can be good without knowledge! Indeed, without knowledge, the heart is worthless. But there is a sort of knowledge that rests in the mere speculation of things, and there is a knowledge that is accompanied by the grace of faith and love, which moves a person to do the will of God from the heart.[e] The first of these will satisfy the talker, but the true Christian is not content without the other. 'Give me understanding, that I may keep your law and observe it with my whole heart.[f]'"

"You're just trying to trap me again," Talkative snapped. "This is not helpful for building anyone up."

"Well, if you like, you can suggest another sign of how this work of grace reveals itself," Faithful offered.

"Not me," said Talkative, "for I see we are not going to agree."

"Well, if you will not, will you give me permission to do it?"

"Do as you please," Talkative replied.

"Others will observe the work of grace in a person through the following: First, by their sincere confession of faith in Christ that comes from personal experience. Second, by a life that matches that confession—that is, a life of holiness. This means holiness in the heart, holiness in the family (if they have one), and holiness in their conduct in the world. Grace transforms a person and leads them to inwardly hate their sin, and to hate their own weaknesses for that matter, in secret. It leads them to suppress sinfulness in their own family and to promote holiness in the world. This is done not by talk alone, as a hypocrite or a talkative person might do, but by a practical submission, in faith and love, to the power of the Word.

And now, sir," Faithful concluded, "that is my brief description of the work of grace and how it is revealed. If you have anything to object to, please object. If not, may I ask you a second question?"

"No, I do not wish to debate just now. I would rather listen," Talkative said. "Let me have your second question."

"It is this," said Faithful. "Have you personally experienced the first part of the description I gave? And does your life and your conduct reflect this work of grace? Or does your religion exist only in words and on your tongue, and not in deed and in truth?" Then he quickly added, "If you choose to answer, please say no more than what you know God above would agree with, and also nothing but what your own conscience can justify. For it is not the one who commends himself who is approved, but the one whom the Lord commends.[g] Besides, to say, 'I am this way or that way,' when your lifestyle and all your neighbors say you are lying, is a great wickedness."

Talkative began to blush, but after recovering himself, he replied, "You are now appealing to experience, to conscience, and to God, and you are appealing to Him to justify what is said. I did not expect this kind of conversation, nor am I inclined to answer such questions, because I do not consider myself obligated to do so. You would have to take it upon yourself to be my catechist, and even if you did, I could still refuse to make you my judge. But please tell me why you ask me such questions?"

"Because I saw how eager you were to talk, and because I suspected you had nothing but idle words," Faithful said. "Besides, to tell you the whole truth, I have heard that you are a man whose religion is all in his talk, and that your lifestyle makes a liar out of your profession of faith. They say you are an embarrassment to the faith because of your ungodly conduct. Some have already stumbled because of your wicked ways, and more are in danger of being destroyed by them. Your supposed religion stands arm-in-arm with alehouses, greed, impurity, swearing, lying, and keeping bad company. The proverb that is said of a prostitute is true of you: that she is a shame to all women. In the same way, you are a shame to all who profess faith."

"Since you are so quick to believe rumors and to judge so rashly, I can only conclude that you are some irritable or depressed man, unfit for conversation," Talkative said. "And so, farewell."

Then Christian came up and said to his brother, "I told you it would happen this way. Your words and his worldly desires could not agree. He would rather leave your company than change his life. Now he is gone, just as I said. Let him go; the loss is no one's but his own. He has saved us the trouble of leaving him, for if he continues as he is—which I suppose he will—he would have been nothing but a stain on our company. Besides, the apostle says, 'Have nothing to do with such people.[h]'"

"But I am glad we had this short conversation with him," Faithful said. "It may encourage him to rethink his views. In any case, I have dealt plainly with him, and so I am innocent of his blood if he perishes."

"You did well to talk so candidly to him," Christian replied. "There is very little of this kind of faithful dealing with people nowadays, and that is what makes religion stink in the nostrils of so many. For it is these talkative fools, whose religion is only in their words and whose lifestyles are corrupt and worldly, who—by being so readily admitted into the fellowship of the godly—confuse the world, tarnish Christianity, and grieve those who are sincere. I wish that everyone would deal with such people as you have done. Then they would either be made to conform to true religion, or the company of saints would become too hot for them."

Then Faithful said:

"See how Talkative at first lifts his plumes!
How bravely does he speak! How he presumes
To drive down all before him! But as soon
As we speak of the heart, then like the moon
That's past its full, into a wane he goes.
And so will all, but he whose heart-work shows."

---

[a] *1Co. 9:24*
[b] *Rom. 2:13*
[c] *Jam. 1:27*
[d] *Mat. 13:23*
[e] *Gal. 5:6*
[f] *Psa. 119:34*
[g] *2Co. 10:18*
[h] *2Ti. 3:5*

Chapter 13: Evangelist's Warning and Vanity Fair

Behold! Evangelist, and all he hath,
Shows to the world the true and perfect path.
The pilgrims' joys, when he comes in their sight,
Are turned to warnings of a dreadful fight.

In this way they travelled together talking about what they had seen, and this made easy what would otherwise have been a tedious part of their journey, for they were now going through a long wilderness.

Now, as they approached the edge of this wilderness, Faithful happened to look back and saw someone coming after them, and he recognized him. "Oh!" said Faithful to his brother. "Look who is that coming over there!" Then Christian looked and said, "It is my good friend Evangelist." "Yes, and my good friend too," said Faithful, "for it was he who set me on the path to the gate." When Evangelist caught up to them, he said, "Peace be with you, dearly beloved, and peace be to all who help you."

"Welcome, welcome, my good Evangelist!" Christian exclaimed. "The sight of your face reminds me of your past kindness and your tireless work for my eternal good."

"And a thousand times welcome!" said good Faithful. "Oh, sweet Evangelist, your company is so desirable to us poor pilgrims!"

Then Evangelist said, "How have things gone with you, my friends, since we last parted? What have you encountered, and how have you conducted yourselves?"

Then Christian and Faithful told him about everything that had happened to them on the way, and how, and with what difficulty, they had arrived at that place.

"I am truly glad," said Evangelist, "not that you have faced trials, but that you have been victorious. And I am glad that despite many weaknesses, you have continued on the path to this very day. I say, I am truly glad about this, both for my own sake and for yours. I have sown, and you have reaped, and the day is coming when 'he who sows and he who reaps will rejoice together.[a]' That is, if you endure, 'for at the proper time we will reap a harvest if we do not give up.[b]'

"The crown is before you, and it is one that will not fade; 'run in such a way as to get the prize.[c]' There are some who set out for this crown and, after they have gone a long way for it, another comes and takes it from them. 'Hold on to what you have, so that no one will take your crown.[d]'

Then Evangelist warned them: "You are not yet out of the devil's range. You have not yet resisted to the point of shedding your blood in your struggle against sin. Let the kingdom always be before you and believe firmly in things that are unseen. Do not let anything from this side of the next world get inside of you.

"And above all, guard your own hearts and their desires, for the heart is 'deceitful above all things and beyond cure.'[e] Set your faces like flint; you have all power in heaven and on earth on your side."

Christian thanked him for his encouragement and asked if he would offer some advice to help them during the rest of the journey. They were especially eager for this because they knew he was a prophet and could tell them of things that might happen to them, and also how they might resist and overcome them. Faithful also agreed to this request. So Evangelist began as follows:

"My sons," Evangelist began, "you have heard in the words of the gospel that you must enter the kingdom of heaven through many tribulations. You have also heard that in every city, bonds and afflictions await you. You cannot expect to go far on a pilgrimage without encountering these difficulties in one form or another. I know you have already experienced some trials, but more will follow shortly."

"As you can see, you are almost out of this wilderness, and you will soon come to a town that you will see before you. In that town, you will be fiercely attacked by enemies who will try to kill you. And be sure of this: one or both of you must seal your commitment with blood. But be faithful unto death, and the King will give you a crown of life.[f]"

"The one who dies there, although his death will be unnatural and his pain perhaps great, will be better off than his companion! Not only will he arrive at the Celestial City sooner, but he will escape many miseries that the other will encounter on the rest of his journey."

Evangelist concluded, "When you come to the town and find that what I have told you has come true, then remember your friend, act like men, and commit the keeping of your souls to your God by doing good, remaining faithful to your Creator."[g]

---

[a] *Jhn. 4:36*
[b] *Gal. 6:9*
[c] *1Co. 9:24-27*
[d] *Rev. 3:11*
[e] *Jer. 17:9*
[f] *Rev. 2:10*
[g] *1Pe. 4:19*

Chapter 14: Vanity Fair

Behold! Vanity Fair, the Pilgrims there
Are chained and stand beside;
Even so it was our Lord passed here,
And on Mount Calvary died.

Then I saw in my dream that when they had gotten out of the wilderness, they immediately saw a town before them, and the name of that town is **Vanity**. In the town, there is a fair that is held, called **Vanity Fair**[1]. It is kept all year long. It bears the name Vanity Fair because the town where it is held is more fleeting and frivolous than vanity itself, and also because everything that is sold there, or that comes there, is vanity. As the wise man says, "Everything to come is vanity.[a]"

This fair is not a new enterprise, but an ancient establishment. It all began almost five thousand years ago, when pilgrims were walking to the Celestial City, just as these two honest men are now. Beelzebub, Apollyon, and Legion, with their companions, saw by the path the pilgrims made that their way to the City lay through this town of Vanity. So they schemed to set up a fair here—a fair where all sorts of vanity would be sold, and one that would last all year long.

All manner of vain merchandise is sold at this fair: houses, lands, trades, positions, honors, promotions, titles, countries, kingdoms, lusts, pleasures, and delights of all sorts, such as prostitutes, pimps, wives, husbands, children, masters, servants, lives, blood, bodies, souls, silver, gold, pearls, precious stones, and so on.

Moreover, at this fair, you can always see juggling, cheats, games, plays, fools, apes, scoundrels, and rogues of every kind.

---

[1] *Vanity Fair is one of Bunyan's most famous allegories. It represents the entire world system, with its endless distractions, temptations, and material pursuits that stand in opposition to the Christian pilgrimage.*

Here you can also see—and for no cost at all—thefts, murders, adulteries, and perjurers; and persecutors who spill the blood of innocents.

Just as other, less important fairs have various rows and streets with their own names where specific wares are sold, so too in this fair you have the proper places—rows, streets, countries, and kingdoms—where the wares of this fair can be most easily found. Here is the Britain Row, the French Row, the Italian Row, the Spanish Row, and the German Row, where different kinds of vanities are sold. But, just as in other fairs where one commodity is the chief attraction, the wares of Rome and her merchandise are greatly promoted in this fair, though the English nation and some others have taken a dislike to them.

Now, as I said, the way to the Celestial City lies right through this town where this bustling fair is held. Anyone who wants to go to the City without going through this town would have to "leave this world."[b] The Prince of Princes Himself went through this town on His way to His own country, and on a day when the Fair was in full swing, no less. And as I recall, it was Beelzebub, the chief lord of this fair, who invited Him to buy his vanities. Indeed, Beelzebub would have made Him lord of the Fair if He would have only paid him reverence as He went through the town.[c] Yes, because He was such a person of honor, Beelzebub took Him from street to street and, in a short time, showed Him all the kingdoms of the world so that he might, if possible, tempt the Blessed One to bargain for and buy some of his vanities.[d] But He had no desire for the merchandise and therefore left the town without spending so much as a single penny on these vanities. This fair, therefore, is an ancient and long-standing institution, and a very great fair indeed.

Now these pilgrims, as I said, had to go through this fair. And so they did. But as soon as they entered, all the people in the Fair were stirred up, and the town itself was in an uproar about them for several reasons.

First, the pilgrims were dressed in clothes that were different from the clothing of anyone who traded in that fair. The people of the Fair, therefore, stared at them. Some said they were fools; some said they were lunatics, and some said they were foreigners.[e]

Second, just as the people wondered at their clothing, they also wondered at their speech, for few could understand what they said. The pilgrims naturally spoke the language of Canaan, but those who ran the Fair were people of this world, so from one end of the Fair to the other, each seemed like a barbarian to the other.[f]

Third, and what especially baffled the merchants, was that these pilgrims placed very little value on all their wares. They didn't even care to look at them. And if the merchants called out to them to buy something, the pilgrims would put their fingers in their ears and cry, "Turn my eyes away from looking at worthless things," and then look upward, signaling that their business was in heaven.[g]

One man, seeing how the pilgrims behaved, happened to say to them mockingly, "What will you buy?" But they, looking at him seriously, answered, "We buy the truth.[h]"[2]

At that, the crowd began to despise the men even more. Some were mocking, some were taunting, some were speaking abusively, and some were calling on others to strike them. At last, things erupted into a great uproar and commotion in the Fair, so much so that all order was lost. Word was immediately brought to the great one of the Fair, who quickly came down and assigned some of his most trusted friends to take these men in for interrogation, as the Fair had nearly been overturned because of them.

So, the men were brought to be examined. Those who sat in judgment asked where they came from, where they were going, and what they were doing there in such unusual clothing.

The pilgrims said that they were pilgrims and strangers in the world and that they were going to their own country, which was the heavenly Jerusalem.[i] They said that they had given no reason for the men of the town or the merchants to abuse them and to hinder them on their journey, except for the fact that when one of them asked what they would buy, they said they would buy the truth.

---

[2] *This famous declaration is the pilgrims' thesis statement against the Fair. It likely references Proverbs 23:23 ("Buy the truth and do not sell it") and shows that they value eternal, divine truth above all worldly goods.*

But those who were appointed to examine the pilgrims did not believe they were anything other than lunatics and madmen, or else people who had come to throw the Fair into confusion. Therefore, they took them and beat them, smeared them with dirt, and then put them in a cage so that they might be made a spectacle for all the people of the Fair.

There they lay for some time and were made the objects of anyone's sport, malice, or revenge, while the great one of the Fair laughed at everything that happened to them. But the men were patient. Instead of returning insults for insults, they offered blessings; they offered good words for bad, and kindness for the injuries they received. Seeing this, some of the people in the Fair who were more observant and less prejudiced than the rest began to scold and blame the wicked ones for their continual abuse of the men.

In response, the wicked ones angrily attacked them as well, counting them as bad as the men in the cage and telling them that they seemed to be conspirators who should share in the pilgrims' misfortunes. The others replied that, from what they could see, the pilgrims were quiet, sober, and intended no one any harm. They added that there were many merchants in their fair who were more worthy of being put into the cage—and the pillory, too—than the men they had abused.

Thus, after various arguments had passed on both sides—with the pilgrims behaving very wisely and soberly the entire time—the townspeople came to blows among themselves and harmed one another. Then these two poor men were brought before their examiners again and were charged with being guilty of the recent uproar in the Fair. So, they beat them mercilessly, put them in chains, and led them up and down the Fair as an example and a terror to others, so that no one would dare speak on their behalf or join them.

But Christian and Faithful behaved themselves even more wisely. They received the disgrace and shame that was cast upon them with so much meekness and patience that they won several of the people in the Fair to their side, though they were few in comparison to the rest. This put the other party into an even greater rage, so much so that they decided on the death of these two men.

Therefore, they decided that neither the cage nor the chains would be enough, but that the pilgrims would die for the trouble they had caused and for deceiving the men of the Fair.

Then they were sent back to the cage again while their jailers awaited further orders. So, they were put in, and their feet were fastened in the stocks.

Here, they once again remembered what they had heard from their faithful friend Evangelist, and they were all the more certain about their circumstances and their sufferings because of his prophecy. They also comforted each other that whoever's fate it was to suffer would have the better outcome. Therefore, each man secretly wished that he might have that honor. So, committing themselves to the all-wise plan of Him who rules all things, they remained content in their situation until their fate was decided.

---

[a] *Ecc. 11:8*
[b] *1Co. 5:10*
[c] *Mat. 4:9*
[d] *Mat. 4:8*
[e] *1Co. 4:9-10*
[f] *1Co. 14:11*
[g] *Phl. 3:20*
[h] *Pro. 23:23*
[i] *Heb. 11:13-16*

Chapter 15: The Trial at Vanity Fair

Now Faithful, play the man, speak for thy God:
Fear not the wicked's malice, nor their rod:
Speak boldly, man, the truth is on thy side;
Die for it, and to life in triumph ride.

Then, at the appointed time, they brought them out for their trial, which was held in order to condemn them. When the time came, they were brought before their enemies and formally charged. The judge's name was Lord **Hate-good**[1]. Their indictment was the same in substance, though it varied slightly in form. The contents were as follows:

"That they were enemies to and disturbers of our trade; that they have caused commotions and divisions in the town; and that they have won a group over to their own most dangerous opinions, in contempt of the law of our prince."

Then Faithful began to answer. He said that he had only opposed that which had set itself against Him who is higher than the highest. "And as for the charge of disturbance," he said, "I have made none, as I am a man of peace. The people who were won over to our side were won by seeing our truth and innocence, and they have only turned from what is worse to what is better. And as for the king you speak of, since he is Beelzebub, the enemy of our Lord, I defy him and all his angels."

Then a proclamation was made that anyone who had anything to say for their lord the king against the prisoner at the bar should come forward immediately and give their evidence. So, three witnesses came in: **Envy**, **Superstition**, and **Pickthank**[2]. They were then asked if they knew the prisoner at the bar and what they had to say for their lord the king against him.

---

[1] *The judge's name is allegorical. It is a common interpretation that Lord Hate-good represents the idea that the worldly legal system, in its fallen state, is inherently hostile to divine goodness and righteousness.*

[2] *A* ***"pickthank"*** *is an archaic term for a sycophant or flatterer—someone who seeks to gain favor (to "pick" up "thanks") by telling tales.*

Then Envy stepped forward and said, "My Lord, I have known this man for a long time, and I will testify under oath before this honorable court that he is—"

"Hold!" the judge interrupted. "Administer the oath." (So they swore him in.) Then Envy continued, "My Lord, this man, despite his plausible-sounding name, is one of the vilest men in our country. He pays no attention to prince or people, law or custom, but does everything he can to fill everyone with his disloyal ideas, which he generally calls 'principles of faith and holiness.' Specifically, I myself once heard him declare that Christianity and the customs of our town of Vanity are diametrically opposed and cannot be reconciled. By saying this, my Lord, he not only condemns all of our praiseworthy activities but condemns us for doing them."

Then the judge said to him, "Do you have anything more to say?"

"My Lord, I could say much more, but I do not wish to be tedious to the court," Envy replied. "After the other gentlemen have given their evidence, if you need anything further to help convict him, I will gladly expand my testimony against him." So Envy was told to stand aside. Then they called **Superstition** and told him to look at the prisoner. They also asked what he could say for their lord the king against him. Then they swore him in, and he began.

"My Lord," Superstition said, "I do not know this man well, nor do I desire to know him any better. However, I do know that he is a very troublesome fellow, based on a conversation I had with him the other day in this town. While talking with him, I heard him say that our religion was worthless and that no one could possibly please God by following it. Your Lordship knows very well what necessarily follows from such sayings: that we worship in vain, that we are still in our sins, and that we will ultimately be damned. And that is what I have to say."

Then **Pickthank** was sworn in and told to say what he knew on behalf of their lord the king against the prisoner at the bar.

"My Lord, and all you gentlemen," Pickthank began, "I have known this fellow for a long time and have heard him say things that should not be said. He has cursed our noble prince Beelzebub and has spoken with contempt about his honorable friends, whose names are the Lord Old Man, the Lord Carnal Delight, the Lord Luxurious, the Lord Desire of

Vain-glory, my old Lord Lechery, and Sir Having Greedy, along with all the rest of our nobility. He has said, moreover, that if all men were of his mind, not one of these noblemen would be allowed to exist in this town any longer. Besides, he has not been afraid to curse you, my Lord, who are now appointed to be his judge, calling you an ungodly villain, along with many other insulting terms with which he has slandered most of the gentry of our town."

When Pickthank had finished his tale, the judge addressed the prisoner at the bar, saying, "You renegade, heretic, and traitor, have you heard what these honest gentlemen have testified against you?"

"May I speak a few words in my own defense?" Faithful asked.

"Sirrah! Sirrah!"[3] the judge shouted. "You deserve to live no longer, but to be killed immediately right here. Yet, so that all may see our gentleness toward you, let us hear what you, vile renegade, have to say."

"First," Faithful began, "in answer to what Mr. Envy has testified, I have never said anything except this: That any rule, law, custom, or people that is directly against the Word of God is diametrically opposed to Christianity. If I have spoken wrongly in this, convince me of my error, and I am ready to make my recantation here before you."

"Second, regarding Mr. Superstition and his charge against me, I said only this: That in the worship of God, a Divine faith is required. But there can be no Divine faith without a Divine revelation of the will of God. Therefore, whatever is injected into the worship of God that does not agree with Divine revelation can only be done by a human faith, and that kind of faith will not lead to eternal life."

"Third, as for what Mr. Pickthank has said, I will say this (while avoiding harsh terms like 'cursing' and so on): the prince of this town and all the rabble of his attendants that this gentleman named are more fit to be in Hell than in this town and country. And so, may the Lord have mercy on me!"

Then the Judge called to the jury (who had been standing by the whole time to listen and observe). "Gentlemen of the jury, you see this

---

[3] ***"Sirrah"*** *is an archaic term of address, used by a person of higher status toward a social inferior (like a servant or, in this case, a prisoner). It was almost always used to express anger, contempt, or a harsh command, highlighting the judge's immediate and baseless scorn for Faithful.*

man about whom such a great uproar has been made in this town. You have also heard what these worthy gentlemen have testified against him. You have also heard his reply and confession. It now rests in your hands to hang him or to save his life. But I think it is appropriate to instruct you in our law.

"There was an Act made in the days of Pharaoh the Great, a servant to our prince, that to prevent those of a contrary religion from multiplying and growing too numerous, their male children should be thrown into the river.[a] There was also an Act made in the days of Nebuchadnezzar the Great, another of his servants, that whoever would not fall down and worship his golden image would be thrown into a fiery furnace.[b] There was also an Act made in the days of Darius that whoever, for a certain time, called upon any god but him would be cast into the lions' den.[c] Now, this rebel has broken the substance of these laws, not only in thought (which cannot be tolerated), but also in word and deed, which is especially intolerable.

"Remember, the law of Pharaoh was based on a mere suspicion to prevent future trouble, with no crime yet committed; but here, a crime *is* apparent. As for the second and third laws, you see that he argues against our religion. And as for treason, he has confessed, and he deserves to die."

Then the jury went out. Their names were Mr. Blind-man, Mr. No-good, Mr. Malice, Mr. Love-lust, Mr. Live-loose, Mr. Heady, Mr. High-mind, Mr. Enmity, Mr. Liar, Mr. Cruelty, Mr. Hate-light, and Mr. Implacable. Each one gave his private verdict against him among themselves, and afterward, they unanimously agreed to find him guilty before the Judge.

And first, among themselves, Mr. Blind-man, the foreman, said, "I see clearly that this man is a heretic." Then Mr. No-good said, "Away with such a fellow from the earth." "Yes," said Mr. Malice, "for I hate the very sight of him." Then Mr. Love-lust said, "I could never stand him." "Nor could I," said Mr. Live-loose, "for he was always condemning my way of life." "Hang him, hang him," said Mr. Heady. "A worthless nobody," said Mr. High-mind. "My heart rises up against him," said Mr. Enmity. "He is a rogue," said Mr. Liar. "Hanging is too good for him," said Mr. Cruelty. "Let's get him out of the way," said Mr. Hate-light.

Then Mr. Implacable said, "Even if I were given the whole world, I could not be reconciled to him. Therefore, let us immediately find him guilty of death."

And so, they did. Therefore, he was immediately condemned to be taken from that place back to the place from which he came, and there to be put to the cruellest death that could be invented.

Therefore, they brought him out to do to him according to their law. First, they whipped him, then they beat him with their fists, then they cut his flesh with knives. After that, they stoned him, then stabbed him with their swords, and last of all, they burned him to ashes at the stake. And so Faithful came to his end.

Now I saw that behind the crowd stood a chariot and a pair of horses, waiting for Faithful. As soon as his enemies had killed him, he was taken up into it and was immediately carried up through the clouds with the sound of a trumpet, by the nearest way to the Celestial Gate.

---

[a] *Exo. 1:22*
[b] *Dan. 3:6*
[c] *Dan. 6:7*

Chapter 16: A New Companion and By-ends

Well, Faithful, thou hast faithfully profest
Unto thy Lord; with whom thou shalt be blest,
When faithless ones, with all their vain delights,
Are crying out under their hellish plights:
Sing, Faithful, sing, and let thy name survive;
For though they killed thee, thou art yet alive!

As for Christian, he had a temporary reprieve and was sent back to prison. He remained there for a time, but He who rules over all things, holding the power of their rage in His own hand, arranged it so that Christian escaped them and went on his way.

Now I saw in my dream that Christian did not go on alone, for there was one whose name was **Hopeful** who joined him. Hopeful had been converted by watching Christian and Faithful's words and behavior during their sufferings at the Fair. Entering into a brotherly promise, he told Christian that he would be his companion. Thus, one man died to bear witness to the truth, and another rose from his ashes to be a companion to Christian on his pilgrimage. This Hopeful also told Christian that there were many other men in the Fair who were planning to follow them when the time was right.

So, I saw that soon after they had gotten out of the Fair, they overtook a man who was going on ahead of them, whose name was **By-ends**[1]. They said to him, "What country are you from, sir? And how far are you going this way?" He told them that he came from the town of **Fair-speech** and that he was going to the Celestial City (but he did not tell them his name).

---

[1] In the 17th century, the term "by-ends" referred to a person's secondary or ulterior motives, usually pursued for personal profit or advantage. For example, a village blacksmith might have been said to attend church so he could meet his religious obligations, but also for the "by-end" of appearing respectable to his customers and thus improving his business. Bunyan masterfully uses this now-archaic term to personify a self-serving approach to religion.

"From Fair-speech!" Christian exclaimed. "Does anything good live there?[a]"

"Yes," said By-ends, "I hope so."

"Please, sir, what should I call you?" Christian asked.

"I am a stranger to you, and you are a stranger to me," By-ends said. "If you are going this way, I will be glad for your company. If not, I must be content to go on alone."

"This town of Fair-speech," Christian said, "I have heard of it. And as I remember, they say it is a wealthy place."

"Yes, I assure you that it is," By-ends replied, "and I have many rich relatives there."

"Please, who are your relatives there, if I may be so bold as to ask?" Christian inquired.

"Almost the whole town," By-ends boasted, "and in particular, my Lord Turn-about, my Lord Time-server, and my Lord Fair-speech, from whose ancestors the town first took its name. Also, Mr. Smooth-man, Mr. Facing-both-ways, and Mr. Anything. The parson of our parish, Mr. Two-tongues, was my mother's brother. And to tell you the truth, I have become a gentleman of high status, yet my great-grandfather was just a simple boatman, who looked one way and rowed another—and I earned most of my wealth through the same occupation."

"Are you a married man?" Christian asked.

"Yes, and my wife is a very virtuous woman—her mother was virtuous as well," By-ends said. "She was the daughter of Lady Feigning, so she comes from a very honorable family. She has reached such a level of sophistication that she knows how to behave with everyone, from princes to peasants. It's true that we differ somewhat in religion from the stricter sort, but only on two small points: first, we never strive against wind and tide; second, we are always most zealous when Religion walks in silver slippers. We love to walk with him in the street if the sun is shining and the people are applauding him."

Then Christian leaned over to his companion, Hopeful, and said, "It occurs to me that this is a man named By-ends from Fair-speech. And if it is, we have as devious a scoundrel in our company as lives in all these parts." "Ask him," said Hopeful. "It seems to me he shouldn't be ashamed of his name." So Christian approached him again and said, "Sir, you talk as if you know more than the rest of the world, and if I'm not mistaken, I suspect you are Mr. By-ends, of Fair-speech?"

"That is not my name," By-ends replied, "but it is indeed a nickname given to me by some who cannot stand me. I must be content to bear it as an insult, just as other good men have borne theirs before me."

"And you never gave people a reason to call you by this name?" Christian asked.

"Never, never!" By-ends insisted. "The worst I ever did to earn this name was that I always had the good fortune to find my judgment seemed to align perfectly with the current trends of the times, whatever they were, and I had the good fortune to profit by it. And if things are thrown at me like this, I will count them as a blessing. The malicious have no reason to load me down with insults on account of it!"

"I thought you were the man I had heard of," Christian said. "And to be honest, I'm afraid this name fits you more accurately than you are willing for us to believe."

"Well, if that's what you want to imagine, I can't help it," By-ends replied. "You will find that I am a pleasant companion if you will still allow me to join you."

"If you want to go with us, you must go against wind and tide, which you have said is against your philosophy," Christian said. "You must also embrace Religion when he is in rags as well as when he is in his silver slippers. And you must stand by him when he is bound in chains, just as you would when he walks the streets to applause."

"You cannot impose your faith upon me," By-ends replied. "Leave me to practice religion in my own way and let me go with you."

"Not one step further," Christian said, "unless you agree to do as we do in the matters I've proposed."

Then By-ends said, "I will never desert my old principles, since they are harmless and profitable. If I cannot go with you, I will have to do as I did before you overtook me: go by myself until someone comes along who will be glad for my company."

Now I saw in my dream that Christian and Hopeful left him and kept their distance ahead of him. But one of them, looking back, saw three men following Mr. By-ends. And as they caught up with him, he gave them a very low bow, and they also gave him a compliment. The men's names were Mr. **Hold-the-world**, Mr. **Money-love**, and Mr. **Save-all**—men that Mr. By-ends had known for a long time. In their youth, they were schoolfellows and were taught by a man named Mr. **Gripe-man**, a schoolmaster in **Love-gain**, which is a market town in the county of **Coveting**, in the north. This schoolmaster taught them the art of getting ahead, whether by violence, cheating, flattery, lying, or by putting on the appearance of religion. And these four gentlemen had mastered so much of their teacher's art that any one of them could have run such a school himself.

Christian and Hopeful leave By-ends behind

---

[a] *Pro. 26:25*

Chapter 17: By-ends and His Companions

No matter, By-ends, of your friends you'll find
The wise man is a knave, the good unkind;
A righteous man to sinners is a snare,
Then go your ways, and seek another fair.

After they had greeted each other, Mr. Money-love said to Mr. By-ends, "Who are those people on the road ahead of us?" (For Christian and Hopeful were still within sight).

"They are a couple of travelers from a distant country who are, in their own way, going on a pilgrimage," By-ends answered.

"Alas! Why didn't they wait so that we could have had their good company?" said Mr. Money-love. "For they, and we, and you, sir, I hope, are all going on a pilgrimage."

"We are indeed," By-ends said. "But the men ahead of us are so rigid and so in love with their own ideas, and they have so little respect for the opinions of others, that no matter how godly a person is, if he does not agree with them in all things, they will throw him right out of their company."

"That is bad," said Mr. **Save-all**, "but we read about some who are 'righteous overmuch,' and such men's rigidity leads them to judge and condemn everyone but themselves. But please tell me, what, and how many, were the things on which you differed?"

"Well, in their headstrong way, they conclude that it is their duty to rush on their journey in all kinds of weather, while I prefer to wait for a fair wind and tide," By-ends said. "They are for risking everything for God all at once, while I am for taking every advantage to secure my life and my property. They are for holding on to their beliefs even if everyone is against them, but I am for religion only when and where the circumstances and my personal safety will allow it. They are for Religion when he is in rags and scorned, but I am for him when he walks in his golden slippers, in the sunshine, and with applause."

"Yes, and you should hold to that position, good Mr. By-ends!" said Mr. Hold-the-world. "For my part, I can only consider a man a fool who, having the freedom to keep what he has, is so unwise as to lose it. Let us be as wise as serpents. It is best to make hay while the sun shines. You see how the bee stays still all winter and only stirs when she can have profit with her pleasure. God sometimes sends rain and sometimes sunshine; if those men ahead are such fools as to go through the rain, let us be content to take the fair weather. For my part, I like the religion that best aligns with the security of God's good blessings to us. For who, if he is ruled by reason, can imagine that God would give us the good things of this life if He didn't want us to keep them for His sake? Abraham and Solomon grew rich in their religion. And Job says that a good man shall lay up gold like dust. But he must be different from the men ahead of us, if they are as you have described them."

"I think we are all agreed on this matter," said Mr. Save-all, "and therefore, nothing more needs to be said about it."

"No, nothing more needs to be said, indeed," said Mr. Money-love. "For anyone who believes neither Scripture nor reason—and you see we have both on our side—neither knows the personal freedom grace affords, nor does he seek his own safety."

"My brothers," said By-ends, "we are, as you see, all going on a pilgrimage. Allow me to divert our attention from negative things and ask a question:

Suppose a man—a minister or a tradesman, for example—has an opportunity before him to gain the good blessings of this life. However, he cannot possibly get them unless, in appearance at least, he becomes extraordinarily zealous in some points of religion that he never bothered with before. May he not use this method to achieve his goal and still be a truly honest man?"

"I see the heart of your question," said Mr. Money-love, "and with these gentlemen's permission, I will offer an answer. First, to speak to your question as it concerns a minister: Suppose a minister, a worthy man, who serves a very small congregation but has his eye on a greater one that is much more prosperous. He now has an opportunity to get it, but only by being more studious, preaching more frequently and zealously, and—

because the mood of the people requires it—by altering some of his principles. For my part, I see no reason why a man may not do this (provided he has a calling), and a great deal more besides, and still be an honest man."

"And here is why:

First, his desire for a larger congregation is lawful (this cannot be contradicted), since it is set before him by Providence. Therefore, he may get it if he can, without any crisis of conscience.

Second, his desire for that position makes him more studious and a more zealous preacher, and so it makes him a better man. Indeed, it makes him improve his skills, which is according to the mind of God.

Third, as for complying with the mood of his people by setting aside some of his principles to serve them, this shows: one, that he has a self-denying temperament; two, that he has a sweet and winning personality; and three, that he is therefore more fit for the ministry.

Fourth, I conclude, then, that a minister who changes a small position for a great one should not be judged as greedy for doing so. Rather, since he has improved his skills and his diligence because of it, he should be seen as one who is pursuing his calling and the opportunity put into his hands to do good."

"And now for the second part of the question, which concerns the tradesman you mentioned. Suppose such a man has but a poor business in the world, but by becoming religious, he can improve his market—perhaps get a rich wife, or more and far better customers for his shop. For my part, I see no reason why this cannot be lawfully done. And here is why:

First, to become religious is a virtue, no matter how a man becomes so.

Second, it is not unlawful to get a rich wife or more customers for my shop.

Third, the man who gets these things by becoming religious gets what is good from those who are good by becoming good himself. So then, here is a good wife, good customers, and good profit—and all of these are gained by becoming religious, which is a good thing. Therefore, to become religious in order to get all these things is a good and profitable plan."

This answer, given by Mr. Money-love to Mr. By-ends's question, was highly applauded by them all. They therefore concluded that it was a most wholesome and advantageous philosophy. And because they thought no one would be able to contradict it, and because Christian and Hopeful were still within shouting distance, **they all agreed** to challenge them with the question as soon as they caught up. They were especially eager to do this because the pilgrims had opposed Mr. By-ends before.

So, they called after them, and Christian and Hopeful stopped and stood still until the group came up to them. But as they walked, they decided that old Mr. Hold-the-world, not Mr. By-ends, should pose the question, because they supposed that the pilgrims' answer to him would be free of the heated feelings that had been stirred up between them and Mr. By-ends when they parted ways a little earlier.

Chapter 18: The Refutation of By-ends

The hypocrite, in worldly wisdom's guise,
Will frame a question full of clever lies.
But Christian's answer, simple, clear, and bold,
Shows truth is better than a mine of gold.

So, the two groups came together, and after a short greeting, Mr. Hold-the-world presented the question to Christian and Hopeful and challenged them to answer it if they could.

Then Christian said, "Even a babe in religion could answer ten thousand such questions. For if it is unlawful to follow Christ for loaves of bread, as it is written in the sixth chapter of John,[a] how much more detestable is it to use Him and religion as a means to get ahead and to secure worldly things! We know of no one except heathens, hypocrites, devils, and witches who are of this opinion."

"First, the heathens. For when Hamor and Shechem desired the daughter and cattle of Jacob and saw that there was no way for them to get them except by being circumcised, they said to their companions, 'If every male among us is circumcised as they are, won't their cattle, their substance, and every one of their animals be ours?' Their goal was the daughter and the cattle, and they used religion as a cover to get them. Read the whole story.[b]"

"Second, the hypocritical Pharisees also embraced this sort of religion. Long prayers were their pretense, but their intent was to take widows' houses, and for this, their judgment from God was a greater damnation.[c]"

"Third, Judas the devil was also of this religion. He was religious for the money bag, so that he might possess what was in it. But he was lost, cast away, and the very son of perdition.[d]"

"Fourth, Simon the sorcerer was of this religion, too, for he wanted to have the Holy Spirit so that he might make money with it, and his sentence from Peter's mouth was fitting.[e]"

"Fifth, it is obvious that any man who takes up religion for the sake of the world will also throw away religion for the sake of the world. For just as surely as Judas gave up the world to become religious, he just as surely sold his religion and his Master for that same world. Therefore, to answer the question affirmatively, as I see you have done, and to accept such an answer as valid, is heathenish, hypocritical, and devilish, and your reward will be according to your works."

Then the men stood staring at one another but had nothing with which to answer Christian. Hopeful also approved of the soundness of Christian's answer, and so there was a great silence among them. Mr. By-ends and his company also **fell back** and kept their distance, so that Christian and Hopeful could get ahead of them.

Then Christian said to his companion, "If these men cannot stand before the judgment of other men, what will they do before the judgment of God? And if they are silent when confronted by vessels of clay, what will they do when they are rebuked by the flames of a devouring fire?"

---

[a] *Jhn. 6:26-27*
[b] *Gen. 34:20-24*
[c] *Luk. 20:46-47*
[d] *Jhn. 12:4-6*
[e] *Act. 8:19-22*

Chapter 19: The Silver Mine of Demas

A silver mine, a pit of endless strife,
A den of thieves, a grave for foolish life;
For Demas' smiles and his enticing call
Have led the greedy to a fatal fall.

Then Christian and Hopeful went on ahead of them again until they came to a pleasant plain called **Ease**, where they walked with great contentment. But that plain was narrow, so they crossed it quickly. Now on the far side of the plain was a little hill called **Lucre**, and in that hill was a silver mine. Some who had previously come this way had turned aside to see it because it was such a rare sight. Among those there were many who, going too near the edge of the pit, had the ground collapse beneath them and were killed. Others had been maimed and were never the same again.

Then I saw in my dream that a little off the road, opposite the silver mine, stood a man named **Demas**, who looked like a gentleman. He was calling out to passersby to come and see, and he said to Christian and his companion, "Hello! Come over here, and I will show you something!"

"What could be so important as to divert us from our path to see it?" Christian asked.

"Here is a silver mine, and some are digging in it for treasure," Demas said. "If you will come over, with just a little effort, you can provide richly for yourselves."

Then Hopeful said, "Let's go see."

"Not me," said Christian. "I have heard of this place before and of how many have been killed here. Besides, treasure is a snare to those who seek it, for it hinders them on their pilgrimage.[a]" Then Christian called to Demas, saying, "Isn't the place dangerous? Hasn't it hindered many on their pilgrimage?"

"It is only dangerous to those who are careless," Demas said, but he blushed as he spoke.

Then Christian turned to Hopeful and said, "Let's not move a single step, but instead keep on our way."

"I guarantee you," said Hopeful, "that when By-ends comes along, if he gets the same invitation we did, he will turn in there to see."

"No doubt about it," Christian replied, "for his principles lead him that way, and it's a hundred-to-one bet that he dies there."

Then Demas called again, saying, "But won't you come over and see?"

Christian turned and responded sharply, "Demas, you are an enemy to the righteous ways of the Lord of this path, and you have already been condemned by one of His Majesty's judges for turning aside.[b] Why are you trying to bring us into the same condemnation? Besides, if we turn aside at all, our Lord and King will certainly hear of it, and He will put us to shame in the very place where we wish to stand boldly before Him."

Demas protested that he was also one of their brotherhood and that if they would wait a little while, he would walk with them.

Then Christian said, "What is your name? Is it not the one I have already called you?"

"Yes, my name is Demas," he said. "I am a son of Abraham."

"I know you," Christian replied. "Gehazi was your great-grandfather, and Judas was your father, and you have walked in their footsteps.[c] This is nothing but a devilish trick you are playing. Your father was hanged for being a traitor, and you deserve no better reward. Rest assured, when we come to the King, we will tell him of your behavior." And with that, they went on their way.

By this time, By-ends and his companions had come back into view, and at the first signal from Demas, they went over to him. Now, I do not know if they fell into the pit while looking over the edge, or they went down to dig, or they suffocated at the bottom from the fumes that commonly arise, but I did observe that they were never seen on the path again. Then Christian sang:

"By-ends and silver Demas both agree; One calls, the other runs, so he can be A sharer in the profit; so, they choose This world, and their own pilgrimage refuse."

---

[a] *Hos. 4:18*
[b] *2Ti. 4:10*
[c] *2Ki. 5:20-27; Mat 26:14-15; Mat 27:3-5*

Chapter 20: Lot's Wife and the River of God

A monument of what you should not be
Stands on the path for every eye to see;
Let Lot's wife be a warning to your soul,
Lest looking back should keep you from your goal.

Now I saw that, just on the other side of this plain, the pilgrims came to a place where an old monument stood beside the highway. They were both concerned by its strange shape, for it seemed to them as if it were a woman who had been transformed into the shape of a pillar. They stood there staring at it for a time, but they could not figure out what to make of it.

At last, Hopeful saw a strange inscription written above its head. But since he was not a scholar, he called to Christian (who was learned) to see if he could figure out the meaning. So Christian came, and after piecing the letters together for a little while, he found that it said, "Remember Lot's Wife.[a]" He read it to his companion, after which they both concluded that this was the pillar of salt that Lot's wife was turned into for looking back with a greedy heart when fleeing from Sodom to safety.[b] This sudden and amazing sight prompted the following conversation.

"Well brother, this is a timely sight!" Christian exclaimed. "It came at the perfect moment, after the invitation Demas gave us to come and see the Hill of Lucre. If we had gone over as he wanted, and as you were inclined to do, my brother, we might have been made into a spectacle, just like this woman, for those who will come after us."

"I am sorry that I was so foolish," Hopeful said, "and I am amazed that I am not now like Lot's wife. For what was the difference between her sin and mine? She only looked back, and I had a desire to go and see. Let grace be praised and let me be ashamed that such a thing was ever in my heart."

"Let us take note of what we see here so it may help us in the future," Christian said. "This woman escaped one judgment, for she did not die in the destruction of Sodom, only to be destroyed by another, as we see that she is turned into a pillar of salt."

"True," Hopeful replied. "And she can be both a warning and an example to us. But I am amazed at one thing: how can Demas and his friends stand over there so confidently, looking for that treasure, when this woman was turned into a pillar of salt merely for looking back at it? The Scripture doesn't even say she stepped off the path. The judgment that overtook her serves as an example right in their line of sight; they could not help but see her if they only lifted their eyes."

"It is a thing to be marveled at, and it proves that their hearts have grown desperate with greed," Christian said. "I can think of no one to compare them to so accurately as to those who pick pockets in the presence of the judge, or who cut purses under the gallows. It is said of the men of Sodom that they were sinners 'exceedingly,' because they were sinners 'before the Lord'[c]—that is, right in His sight—despite the kindness He had shown them, for the land of Sodom was like the Garden of Eden at that time.[d] This, therefore, provoked His jealousy all the more and made their plague as hot as the fire of the Lord from heaven could make it. And it is most logical to conclude that those who sin in God's sight, and in spite of such examples that are continually set before them as a warning, must receive the most severe judgments."

"Without a doubt, you have spoken the truth," Hopeful said. "But what a mercy it is that neither of us—but especially me—was made into this example! This gives us reason to thank God, to fear before Him, and to always remember Lot's wife."

I saw then that they went on their way to a pleasant river, which King David called "the river of God," but John called "the river of the water of life.[e]" Now their path lay right along the bank of the river, so Christian and his companion walked there with great delight. They also drank the water of the river, which was pleasant and invigorating to their weary spirits. Besides this, on both banks of the river, there were green trees that bore all kinds of fruit, and the leaves of the trees were good for medicine. They were also very delighted with the fruit of these trees, and they ate the leaves to prevent illnesses and other diseases that happen to those who get overheated from their travels.[f] On each side of the river there was also a meadow, beautifully adorned with lilies, and it was green all year long. In this meadow they lay down and slept, for here they could rest safely.[g]

When they awoke, they again gathered the fruit from the trees, drank again from the water of the river, and then lay down again to sleep. They did this for several days and nights. Then they sang:

"Behold how these crystal streams do glide,
To comfort pilgrims by the highway side.
The meadows green, with their fragrant smell,
Yield delicacies; and he who can tell
What pleasant fruit and leaves these trees do yield,
Will soon sell all he has to buy this field."

So, when they were ready to go on (for they were not yet at their journey's end), they ate and drank and departed.

---

[a] *Luk. 17:32*
[b] *Gen. 19:26*
[c] *Gen. 13:13*
[d] *Gen. 13:10*
[e] *Psa. 65:9; Rev 22:1; Eze 47:1-12*
[f] *Rev. 22:2*
[g] *Psa. 23:2; Isa 14:30*

Chapter 21: By-Path Meadow and Giant Despair

The pilgrims now, to gratify the flesh,
Will seek its ease; but oh! how they afresh
Do thereby plunge themselves in new griefs;
Who seek to please the flesh, themselves undo.

Now I saw in my dream that they had not journeyed far before the path began to veer away from the river, and this left both of them very sorry, but they did not dare to leave the path. The way leading from the river was rough, and their feet were tender from their travels, and the pilgrims became discouraged in their souls because of the difficulty.[a] As they went on, they kept wishing for a better way.

Now, a little ahead of them, there was a meadow on the left side of the road and a set of steps to get over the fence into it. That meadow was called **By-Path Meadow**[1]. Then Christian said to his companion, "If this meadow lies alongside our path, let's go over into it." He went to the steps to see, and there was a path on the other side of the fence that ran right alongside the road. "This is just what I wished for," said Christian. "This is the easiest walking. Come on, good Hopeful, let's go over."

"But what if this path leads us out of the way?" Hopeful asked.

"That's not likely," said Christian. "Look, doesn't it go right alongside the road?" So Hopeful, being persuaded by his companion, followed him over the steps. When they had crossed over and were on the path, they found it was very easy on their feet. Looking ahead, they saw a man walking as they were, and his name was **Vain-confidence**. They called after him and asked him where that path led. He said, "To the Celestial Gate."

---

[1] *By-Path Meadow represents the temptation to deviate from the difficult, ordained path of Christian living in favor of a way that seems easier from a human perspective. The story illustrates that the moment a believer realizes they have knowingly strayed from God's way, the immediate spiritual consequence is a deep, paralyzing doubt and hopelessness. This state is personified by Giant Despair and his home, Doubting Castle.*

"Look," said Christian, "didn't I tell you so? By this, you can see we are on the right path." So they followed, and he went on ahead of them.

But then night fell, and it grew so dark that none of them could see the man in front of them.

Vain-confidence, the one who went ahead, could not see the way before him and fell into a deep pit.[b] The pit had been made there on purpose by the prince of those grounds to catch vain-glorious fools, and Vain-confidence was dashed to pieces by his fall.

Now Christian and his companion heard him fall. They called out to find out what had happened, but there was no one to answer—only the sound of groaning. Then Hopeful said, "Where are we now?" His companion was silent, fearing that he had led him out of the way. And now it began to rain, thunder, and lightning in a dreadful manner, and the water began to rise quickly.

Then Hopeful groaned to himself, saying, "Oh, if only I had stayed on the path!"

"Who could have thought that this path would lead us out of the way?" Christian lamented.

"I was afraid of it from the very first," said Hopeful, "and that is why I gave you that gentle warning. I would have spoken more plainly, but you are older than I am."

"Brother Hopeful, do not be upset with me," Christian said. "I am sorry I have brought you out of the way and put you in such great danger. Please, my brother, forgive me. I did not do it with evil intent."

"Be comforted, my brother, for I forgive you," said Hopeful. "And believe me, this will turn out for our good."

"I am glad to have such a merciful brother with me," Christian said. "But we must not stand here. Let us try to go back."

"Allow me to go first, brother," Hopeful said.

"No, please let me go first," said Christian, "so that if there is any danger, I will face it first, because it was due to my actions that we both went out of the way."

"No," said Hopeful, "you will not go first, for your mind is troubled, and you may lead us out of the way again." Then, for their encouragement, they heard a voice saying, "Set your heart toward the highway, the way by which you came. Turn back.[c]" But by this time the waters had risen greatly, which made the way back very dangerous. (At that, it occurred to me that it is far easier to wander off the path than it is to find your way back.)

Nonetheless, they ventured back. But it was so dark, and the flood was so high that they nearly drowned nine or ten times.

With all the skill they had, they still could not get back to the steps that night. At last, finding a little shelter, they sat down there until daybreak. But being weary, they fell asleep.

Now, not far from the place where they lay, there was a castle called **Doubting Castle**, and its owner was **Giant Despair**. It was on his grounds that they were now sleeping. The giant came out early in the morning and was walking through his fields when he caught Christian and Hopeful asleep on his land.

With a grim and hostile voice, he told them to wake up and asked them where they were from and what they were doing on his grounds. They told him they were pilgrims and that they had lost their way. Then the Giant said, "You have trespassed against me tonight by trampling and lying on my grounds, and therefore you must come with me."

So they were forced to go, because he was stronger than they were. They also had little to say for themselves, for they knew they were at fault.

The Giant drove them before him and put them into his castle in a very dark dungeon that was nasty and stank to the spirits of these two men.[d] Here they lay from Wednesday morning until Saturday night without a single bit of bread, a drop of drink, or any light, or anyone to ask how they were doing. They were in a terrible state, far from friends and acquaintances. And in this place, Christian had double the sorrow, because it was through his own foolish advice that they had been brought into this distress.

---

[a] *Num. 21:4*
[b] *Isa. 9:16*
[c] *Jer. 31:21*
[d] *Psa. 88:18*

Chapter 22: Doubting Castle

The pilgrims now, to gratify the flesh,
Will seek its ease; but oh! how they afresh
Do thereby plunge themselves in new griefs;
Who seek to please the flesh, themselves undo.

Now, Giant Despair had a wife, and her name was **Diffidence**.[1] When he had gone to bed, he told his wife what he had done—that he had taken a couple of prisoners and thrown them into his dungeon for trespassing on his grounds. Then he asked her what he should do to them next. She asked him who they were, where they came from, and where they were headed, and he told her. Then she advised him that when he got up in the morning, he should beat them without any mercy.

So, when he got up, he took a heavy crab-tree club, went down into the dungeon to them, and first began yelling at them as if they were dogs, although they never said a disrespectful word to him. Then he fell upon them and beat them so terribly that they were not able to tend their wounds or even turn over on the floor. After this, he left them there to lament their misery and mourn in their distress. So they spent that entire day doing nothing but sighing and making bitter laments.

The next night, after talking with her husband about them further and understanding that they were still alive, she advised him to counsel them to kill themselves. So when morning came, the giant went to them in a hostile manner as before. Seeing that they were badly bruised and in pain from the beatings he had given them the day before, he told them that since they were never going to get out of that place, their only option was to immediately take their own lives, either with a knife, a rope, or poison. "For why," he said, "should you choose life, seeing that it is filled with so much bitterness?"

---

[1] In the 17th century, "diffidence" did not mean shyness or timidity, but rather distrust, suspicion, and a lack of faith. As the wife of Giant Despair, she represents the voice of distrust in God's goodness and promises, which is what fuels and encourages a state of despair.

But they begged him to let them go. At that, he gave them an ugly look and, rushing at them, would have undoubtedly made an end of them himself, but he suddenly fell into one of his fits (for he sometimes fell into sudden convulsions in sunny weather) and for a time lost the use of his hands. Therefore, he withdrew and left them as they were to consider what to do.

Then the prisoners began to discuss whether it was best to follow his advice:

"Brother," said Christian, "what can we do? The life we are living now is miserable. For my part, I don't know whether it is better to live like this or to die immediately. 'My soul chooses strangling and death rather than my life,' and the grave is more comforting to me than this dungeon.[a] Should we do as the Giant says?"

"Yes, Christian, our present condition is dreadful," Hopeful said, "and death would be far more welcome to me than to remain like this forever. But let us remember that the Lord of the country to which we are going has said, 'You shall not murder.' This of course applies to another person, but we are even more forbidden to take the Giant's advice and kill ourselves. Remember that he who kills another can only murder his body, but to kill oneself is to kill both body and soul at once. And furthermore, my brother, you talk of ease in the grave, but have you forgotten Hell, where unrepentant murderers certainly go? For 'no murderer has eternal life abiding in him.'"[b]

"Let us not forget that all power is not in the hand of Giant Despair. Others, from what I understand, have been taken by him just as we have, and yet have escaped. Who knows? Perhaps the God who made the world will cause Giant Despair to die, or at some time in the future he may forget to lock us in. Or perhaps he will have another of his fits in front of us and lose the use of his limbs. If that should ever happen again, I for one intend to summon all of my courage and try with all my strength to break free from him. I was a fool for not trying to do it before!

But in any case, my brother, let us be patient and endure for a while. The time may come that gives us a happy release but let us not be our own murderers."

With these words, Hopeful managed to calm his brother's mind for the time being. So, they remained together in the dark that day, in their sad and sorrowful condition.

Well, toward evening, the Giant went down into the dungeon again to see if his prisoners had taken his advice. But when he got there, he found them alive—and "alive" was all they were, for between the lack of bread and water and the wounds they had received from his beating, they could do little more than breathe. But, as I said, he found them alive. This discovery caused him to fall into a terrible rage, and he told them that since they had disobeyed his counsel, it would be worse for them than if they had never been born.

At this, they trembled greatly, and I think Christian fainted. But after coming to his senses again, they renewed their conversation about the Giant's counsel and whether it would be best to take it. Christian again seemed to be in favor of doing it, but Hopeful offered his second reply as follows:

"My brother," he said, "don't you remember how courageous you have been in the past? Apollyon could not crush you, nor could all that you heard, saw, or felt in the Valley of the Shadow of Death. What hardship, terror, and dismay you have already gone through! Have you become nothing but fear? You can see that I am in the dungeon with you, and I am a man far weaker by nature than you are. This Giant has wounded me just as he has wounded you, and has also cut off my bread and water, and I mourn with you here in the darkness. But let us exercise a little more patience. Remember how you acted with courage at Vanity Fair and were not afraid of the chain, the cage, or even a bloody death. Therefore, let us—at least to avoid the shame that is not fitting for a Christian—bear up with patience as well as we can."

Now, when night came again and the Giant and his wife were in bed, she asked him about the prisoners and if they had taken his advice. He replied, "They are stubborn rogues. They would rather bear all hardship than kill themselves."

Then she said, "Take them into the castle yard tomorrow and show them the bones and skulls of those you have already killed. Make them believe that before the week is over, you will also tear them to pieces, just as you have done to their companions before them."

So when the morning came, the Giant went to them again, took them into the castle yard, and showed them the bones, as his wife had told him to do. "These were pilgrims once, just as you are," he said, "and they trespassed on my grounds, just as you have done. And when I saw fit, I tore them to pieces, and within ten days, I will do the same to you. Go on, get down to your den again." And with that, he beat them all the way there. They lay, therefore, all day on Saturday in a miserable state, just as before.

Now, when night had come and Mrs. Diffidence and her husband, the Giant, had gone to bed, they began to talk again about their prisoners. The old Giant wondered aloud why he could not persuade them to kill themselves, neither by his beatings nor with his threats. His wife replied, "I am afraid that they live in the hope that someone will come to rescue them, or perhaps they have lock-picks with them, by which they hope to escape." "Is that what you think, my dear?" said the Giant. "I will search them in the morning."

Well, on Saturday, about midnight, they began to pray and continued in prayer until almost daybreak.

Now, a little before it was day, good Christian, as if suddenly stunned, burst out in a passionate speech: "What a fool I am," he said, "to lie here in a stinking dungeon when I could just as well be walking free! I have a key in my shirt called **Promise**[2] that will, I am convinced, open any lock in Doubting Castle." Then Hopeful said, "That is good news! Good brother, pull it out of your shirt and try it."

---

[2] *It is a consensus among scholars that the Key of Promise represents faith in God's specific promises found in Scripture. It is the ultimate answer to the doubt and despair that imprison the pilgrims, as it is a tool given by God that can unlock any prison of their own making.*

Then Christian pulled the key from his shirt and began to try it on the dungeon door. As he turned the key, the bolt slid back, and the door flew open with ease, and Christian and Hopeful both came out. Then he went to the outer door that leads into the castle yard, and he opened that door with his key as well. After that, he went to the iron gate, for that also had to be opened. That lock was terribly hard to turn, yet the key finally opened it. Then they thrust open the gate to make their escape with speed. But as the gate opened, it made such a loud creaking that it woke Giant Despair. The giant rose hastily to pursue his prisoners but felt his limbs fail him, for his fits took him again, so that he was unable to pursue them. Then they went on and came to the King's Highway again, and so they were safe, because they were out of his territory.

Now, when they were back over the steps, they began to plan what they should do at that spot to prevent those who came after them from falling into the hands of Giant Despair. So, they agreed to erect a pillar there and to engrave this sentence on its side: "Over these steps is the way to Doubting Castle, which is kept by Giant Despair, who despises the King of the Celestial Country and seeks to destroy His holy pilgrims." Because of this, many who followed after read what was written and escaped the danger. After this was done, they sang:

"Out of the way we went, and then we found
What it was like to walk on forbidden ground.
And let all those who follow have a care,
Lest carelessness should lead them to a snare,
And they become the prisoners of Despair,
Whose Doubting Castle waits to trap them there."

---

[a] *Job. 7:15*
[b] *1Jn. 3:15*

CHAPTER 23: THE DELECTABLE MOUNTAINS

The pilgrims now ascend the mountain crest,
Where Shepherds offer them a place to rest.
They show them wonders, give them words of care,
To keep them safe by faith and holy fear.

They went on until they came to the **Delectable Mountains**.[1] These mountains belonged to the Lord of the hill we have spoken of before. So, they went up into the mountains to see the gardens, orchards, vineyards, and fountains of water. There they also drank, washed themselves, and ate freely from the vineyards. Now, on the tops of these mountains, there were Shepherds feeding their flocks, and they stood by the side of the highway.

The pilgrims walked over to them and, leaning on their staffs (as weary pilgrims often do when they stop to talk with someone along the way), they asked, "Whose Delectable Mountains are these? And whose sheep are these that feed upon them?"

"These mountains are Immanuel's Land, and they are within sight of his city," the Shepherds answered. "And the sheep are his also; he laid down his life for them.[a]"

"Is this the way to the Celestial City?" Christian asked.

"You are on the right path," they replied.

"How far is it from here?"

"Too far for anyone except those who will actually make it there."

"Is the way safe or dangerous?" Christian asked.

"It is safe for those for whom it is meant to be safe," they answered, "but 'transgressors stumble in it.'"[b]

"Is there any relief in this place for pilgrims who are weary and faint from the journey?"

---

[1] *The Delectable Mountains represent a place of spiritual maturity and rest, where pilgrims are cared for by the leaders of the established Church. The Shepherds (named Knowledge, Experience, Watchful, and Sincere) personify the ideal qualities of faithful pastors, whose role is to nourish, guide, and protect God's flock.*

"The Lord of these mountains has given us a command 'to show hospitality to strangers,'[c] so everything good this place has to offer is available to you."

I also saw in my dream that when the Shepherds realized they were travelers, they asked them questions: "Where did you come from? How did you get on this path? And by what means have you persevered on it? For few of those who set out to come here ever show their faces on these mountains." The pilgrims answered as they had in other places, and when the Shepherds heard their answers, they were pleased with them and looked very lovingly upon the pilgrims, saying, "Welcome to the Delectable Mountains."

The Shepherds, whose names were **Knowledge**, **Experience**, **Watchful,** and **Sincere**, took them by the hand, led them to their tents, and had them share in the food that was ready. They said, moreover, "We would like you to stay here for a while to get acquainted with us, and also to refresh yourselves with the good things of these Delectable Mountains." The pilgrims then told them that they would be happy to stay. Then they retired to bed for the night, because it was very late.

---

[a] *Jhn. 10:11*
[b] *Hos. 14:9*
[c] *Heb. 13:2*

Chapter 24: The Wonders of the Delectable Mountains

The pilgrims on the mountains take their stand,
To see the wonders of Immanuel's Land.
But what they see fills them with hope and dread,
A glimpse of grace, a vision of the dead.

Then I saw in my dream that in the morning, the Shepherds called Christian and Hopeful to walk with them in the mountains. So they went out with them and walked for a while, enjoying the pleasant views on every side. Then the Shepherds said to one another, "Shall we show these pilgrims some wonders?" After agreeing to do so, they first took them to the top of a hill called **Error**, which was very steep on the far side, and told them to look down to the bottom. So Christian and Hopeful looked down and saw at the bottom several men who had been dashed to pieces by a fall from the top.

Then Christian asked, "What does this mean?"

The Shepherds answered, "Have you not heard of those who were led into error by listening to Hymeneus and Philetus concerning the faith of the resurrection of the body?[a]" They answered, "Yes." Then the Shepherds said, "Those you see lying dashed to pieces at the bottom of this mountain are them. And they have remained unburied to this day, as you see, as an example to others to be careful how they climb too high or how they come too near the edge of this mountain."

Then I saw that they took them to the top of another mountain, named **Caution**, and told them to look into the distance. When they did, they saw what they thought were several men walking up and down among the tombs there. They could see that the men were blind because they sometimes stumbled over the tombs and because they could not find their way out from among them. Then Christian asked, "What does this mean?"

The Shepherds answered, "Did you not see, a little below these mountains, a set of steps that led into a meadow on the left side of this path?" They answered, "Yes." Then the Shepherds said, "From those steps, a path leads directly to Doubting Castle, which is kept by Giant Despair. These men you see among the tombs were once on pilgrimage, just as you are now, until they came to those very steps. And because the right way was rough in that place, they chose to leave it and go into that meadow. There they were taken by Giant Despair and thrown into Doubting Castle. After they had been kept in the dungeon for a while, he finally put out their eyes and led them among these tombs, where he has left them to wander to this very day, so that the saying of the wise man might be fulfilled: 'Whoever wanders from the way of understanding will rest in the assembly of the dead.[b]'"

Then Christian and Hopeful looked at each other with tears gushing from their eyes, but they said nothing to the Shepherds.

Then I saw in my dream that the Shepherds took them to another place, a low area where there was a door in the side of a hill. They opened the door and told the pilgrims to look in. They looked in and saw that it was very dark and smoky inside. They also thought they heard a rumbling noise like a fire and the cries of people being tormented, and they smelled the scent of sulfur.

Then Christian asked, "What does this mean?"

The Shepherds told them, "This is a side path to Hell, a way that hypocrites enter—namely, those who sell their birthright, like Esau; those who sell their master, like Judas; those who blaspheme the gospel, like Alexander; and those who lie and deceive, like Ananias and his wife Sapphira."

Then Hopeful said to the Shepherds, "I see that every one of these people had the appearance of being on a pilgrimage, just as we do now. Is that not so?"

"Yes," the Shepherds answered, "and they kept up that appearance for a long time, too."

"How far were they able to go on their pilgrimage in their time, before they were so miserably cast away?" Hopeful asked.

"Some made it farther, and some not as far as these mountains."

Then the pilgrims said to one another, "We must cry out to the Strong One for strength."

"Yes," said the Shepherds, "and when you receive that strength, you will certainly need to use it."

By this time, the pilgrims wanted to go forward, and the Shepherds wanted them to as well, so they walked together toward the end of the mountains. Then the Shepherds said to one another, "Let us show the pilgrims the gates of the Celestial City, if they have the skill to look through our spyglass." The pilgrims lovingly accepted the offer. So, the Shepherds took them to the top of a high hill called **Clear** and gave them their spyglass to look.

They tried to look, but the memory of the last thing the Shepherds had shown them made their hands shake. Because of this, they could not look steadily through the spyglass, yet they thought they saw something that looked like the gate, and also some of the glory of the place. Then they went away and sang this song:

"Thus, by the Shepherds, secrets are revealed,
Which from all other people are concealed.
Come to the Shepherds, then, if you would see,
Things deep, things hidden, and of mystery."

When they were about to leave, one of the Shepherds gave them a map of the way. Another told them to beware of the Flatterer. The third told them to be careful not to sleep on the Enchanted Ground. And the fourth wished them Godspeed. And with that, I awoke from my dream.

---

[a] *2Ti. 2:17-18*
[b] *Pro. 21:16*

Chapter 25: Ignorance and the Story of Little-Faith

The man of conceit will find his final fall,
Though on the name of Jesus he may call;
He enters not the gate, but climbs the wall,
And so is doomed to perish, once for all.

And I slept, and dreamed again, and I saw the same two pilgrims going down the mountains along the highway toward the City. Now, a little below these mountains, on the left side, lies the country of **Conceit**. From that country, a little crooked lane leads into the path on which the pilgrims were walking. Here, therefore, they met with a very energetic young man who came out of that country, and his name was **Ignorance**.[1] So Christian asked him what region he came from and where he was going.

"Sir, I was born in the country that lies over there, a little on the left, and I am going to the Celestial City," Ignorance said.

"But how do you expect to get in at the gate?" Christian asked. "For you may have some difficulty there."

"The same way other people do," he said.

"But what do you have to show at that gate that will cause it to be opened for you?"

"I know my Lord's will, and I have lived a good life," Ignorance answered. "I pay everyone what I owe them. I pray, fast, pay tithes, and give to charity, and I have left my country for the place where I am going."

"But you did not come in through the wicket-gate that is at the start of this path," Christian said. "You came in here through that same

---

[1] *According to scholars, Ignorance represents a person who insists their salvation is secured by their own good works and sincere intentions. He is "ignorant" of the core gospel concepts of original sin and the need for justification by faith in Christ's righteousness alone.*

crooked lane. Therefore, I am afraid that no matter what you may think of yourself, when the day of reckoning comes, you will be charged with being a thief and a robber, instead of being granted entrance into the City."

"Gentlemen, you are complete strangers to me; I don't know you," Ignorance said. "Be content to follow the religion of your country, and I will follow the religion of mine. I hope everything will be all right. And as for the gate you're talking about, the whole world knows that it is a great distance from our country. I don't think anyone in our region even knows the way to it, nor do they need to worry about it, since we have, as you can see, a fine, pleasant, green lane that comes down from our country as a shortcut onto the path."

When Christian saw that the man was "wise in his own eyes," he said to Hopeful in a whisper, "'There is more hope for a fool than for him.[a]' And moreover, 'Even when a fool walks along the road, he lacks sense, and he says to everyone that he is a fool.[b]' Should we talk further with him, or should we go on ahead for now and leave him to think about what he has already heard? Then we can stop for him again later and see if, by degrees, we can do any good for him."

Then Hopeful said:

"Let Ignorance now think a little while on what's been said, and not with a false smile Refuse good counsel, lest he still remain Unknowing of the truest, greatest gain. God says that those who have no sense at all, Though He has made them, will not escape their fall."[c]

Hopeful added, "I don't think it is good to say everything to him at once. Let's pass him by, if you agree, and talk to him again later, when he is able to handle it."

So they both went on, and Ignorance followed behind them. When they had passed him by a little way, they entered a very dark lane, where they met a man whom seven devils had bound with seven strong cords.[d] They were carrying him back to the door that they had seen in the side of the hill. Now good Christian began to tremble, and so did his companion, Hopeful. Yet as the devils led the man away, Christian looked to see if he knew him, and he thought it might be a man named **Turn-away**, who lived in the town of **Apostasy**. But he could not see his face perfectly, for the man hung his head like a thief who has been caught. After they had passed, Hopeful looked after him and saw a paper on his back with this inscription: "Wicked Professor and Damnable Apostate."

Then Christian said to his companion, "Now I remember something I was told about a good man who lived around here. The man's name was **Little-faith**[2], but he was a good man, and he lived in the town of **Sincere**. This is what happened: at the entrance to this passage, there is a lane that comes down from **Broad-way Gate** called **Dead Man's Lane**, so-called because of the murders that are often committed there. This Little-faith, going on his pilgrimage just as we are now, happened to sit down there and fall asleep.

At that time, three sturdy rogues happened to come down the lane from Broad-way Gate. Their names were **Faint-heart**, **Mistrust**, and **Guilt** (three brothers). Seeing Little-faith where he was, they came galloping up to him. The good man had just woken up and was getting up to continue his journey. So, they all came up to him and, with threatening language, ordered him to stand still."

At this, Little-faith turned as white as a sheet and had no power to either fight or run. Then Faint-heart said, "Hand over your purse." But Little-faith was in no hurry to do it (for he was reluctant to lose his money). So, Mistrust ran up to him, thrust his hand into his pocket, and pulled out a bag of silver. Then Little-faith cried out, "Thieves! Thieves!" With that, Guilt, with a great club in his hand, struck Little-faith on the head and knocked him flat to the ground. He lay there bleeding, as if he would bleed to death.

All this time the thieves stood by. But at last, hearing that someone was on the road and fearing it might be a man named **Great-grace**, who lives in the city of **Good-confidence**, they took off running and left the good man to fend for himself. After a while, Little-faith came to his senses and, getting up, managed to scramble on his way. That was the story.

---

[2] *Little-faith is an allegorical figure representing a genuine believer who has weak faith. The story illustrates that while such a person can be easily overcome by external trials and lose their comfort and joy (their "spending money"), their ultimate salvation (their "jewels") is eternally secure.*

"But did they take everything he had?" Hopeful asked.

"No," Christian replied. "They never searched the place where he kept his jewels, so he still had those. But I was told the good man was deeply troubled by his loss, because the thieves got most of his spending money. What they didn't get, as I said, were his jewels. He also had a little spare change left, but it was barely enough to get him to his journey's end. In fact, if I was told correctly, he was forced to beg as he went to keep himself alive, because he could not sell his jewels. But, between begging and doing what he could, he traveled with a hungry stomach for most of the rest of the way."

"But isn't it a wonder that they didn't get his certificate from him, the one he needed to be admitted at the Celestial Gate?" Hopeful asked.

"It is a wonder," Christian agreed, "but they did not get it, though it wasn't because of any cleverness on his part. He was so stunned by their attack that he had neither the power nor the skill to hide anything. So it was more by good Providence than by his own effort that they missed that good thing."

"But it must have been a great comfort to him that they did not get his jewels," Hopeful said.

"It might have been a great comfort to him if he had used it as he should have," Christian replied. "But those who told me the story said that he made little use of that comfort for the rest of the way, because of the despair he felt from having his money taken. Indeed, he forgot about his jewels for a great part of the rest of his journey. Besides, whenever they did come to his mind and he began to be comforted by them, fresh thoughts of his loss would come back, and those thoughts would swallow up all his comfort."

"Alas, poor man!" said Hopeful. "This must have been a great grief to him."

"Grief? Yes, a grief indeed," Christian replied. "Wouldn't it have been for any of us, to be robbed and wounded in a strange place as he was? It's a wonder he didn't die of grief, poor soul. I was told that for almost the rest of the way, he filled the path with nothing but sorrowful and bitter complaints, telling everyone he met where he was robbed, how it happened, who did it, what he lost, how he was wounded, and that he barely escaped with his life.[e]"

"But it is a wonder that his need did not drive him to sell or pawn some of his jewels so that he could support himself on his journey," Hopeful said.

"You talk like someone who is still a baby chick with a shell on his head," Christian replied. "Why would he pawn them, or to whom would he sell them? In the entire country where he was robbed, his jewels were considered worthless. Nor was the relief they could have provided what he truly needed. Besides, if his jewels had been missing at the gate of the Celestial City, he would have been excluded from his inheritance there, and he knew it. That would have been worse to him than the attack and villainy of ten thousand thieves."

"Why are you so harsh, my brother?" Hopeful asked. "Esau sold his birthright for a single meal of stew, and that birthright was his greatest jewel. If he could do it, why couldn't Little-faith do so too?"[f]

"It is true that Esau sold his birthright, and many others do as well, and by doing so they exclude themselves from the main blessing, just as that wicked man did," Christian explained. "But you must see the difference between Esau and Little-faith, and also between their possessions. Esau's birthright was a symbol of a future promise, but Little-faith's jewels were not. Esau's god was his stomach, but Little-faith's was not. Esau's need was in his fleshly appetite, but Little-faith's was not.

Besides, Esau could see no further than the fulfillment of his lusts. 'Look, I am about to die,' he said, 'so what good is the birthright to me?[g]' But Little-faith, though it was his fate to have only a little faith, was kept by that little faith from such extreme actions. It made him see and value his jewels more than to sell them as Esau did his birthright."

"You have never read anywhere that Esau had faith—not even a little," Christian continued. "Therefore, it is no wonder that when the flesh is in complete control, as it is in a person with no faith to resist it, he will sell his birthright, his soul, and everything else to the devil. For such people are like a donkey in heat, who cannot be turned away.[h] When their minds are set on their lusts, they will have them, no matter the cost.

But Little-faith was of a different nature. His mind was on divine things; he lived on things that were spiritual and from above. Therefore, why would a man of such a nature sell his jewels—even if there had been anyone who would buy them—just to fill his mind with empty things? Will a man trade a day's wages for a bowl full of grass? Can you persuade a turtledove to live on rotting meat like a crow? Though faithless people can pawn, mortgage, or sell everything they have—and themselves along with it—for the sake of their worldly desires, those who have saving faith, even just a little of it, cannot do so. And that, my brother, is where you are mistaken."

"I acknowledge my mistake," Hopeful said, "but your harsh reply almost made me angry."

"Why, I only compared you to one of those lively young birds that runs all over the place with the shell still on its head," Christian replied. "But let's put that aside and consider the matter we were debating, and all will be well between us."

"But Christian," Hopeful said, "I am convinced in my heart that those three fellows are just a bunch of cowards. Otherwise, do you think they would have run as they did at the sound of someone coming down the road? Why didn't Little-faith summon more courage? It seems to me he could have stood up to them for at least one skirmish and only surrendered when there was no other choice."

"Many people claim those thieves are cowards, but few who have actually faced them have found that to be true," Christian replied. "As for great courage, Little-faith had none. And I can tell, my brother, that if it had been you, you would have only put up a short fight before surrendering. And truly, since that is the extent of your appetite for a fight now while they are far away, if they were to appear before you as they did to him, it might make you think twice."

"But consider this also: they are just apprentice thieves. They serve under the king of the bottomless pit, who, if necessary, will come to their aid himself, and his voice is like the roaring of a lion,[i]" Christian said. "I myself have been attacked just as Little-faith was, and I found it to be a terrible thing. Those three villains set upon me, and when I began to resist like a Christian, they just gave a call, and in came their master. I would have, as the saying goes, sold my life for a penny, but as God would have it, I was clothed with battle-tested armor. Yes, and even though I was so well-armed, I found it hard work to fight like a man. No one can know what we face in that kind of combat except for someone who has been in the battle himself."

"And yet you see that they ran when they only supposed that Great-grace was on the road," Hopeful pointed out.

"True, they have often fled, both they and their master, whenever Great-grace has so much as appeared—and no wonder, for he is the King's champion," Christian replied. "But surely you see a difference between Little-faith and the King's champion. Not all the King's subjects are His champions, nor can they all perform such feats of war as he can when they are tested. Is it reasonable to think that a small child could handle Goliath as David did? Or that a wren should have the strength of an ox? Some are strong, and some are weak. Some have great faith, and some have little. This man was one of the weak, and that is why he was overcome."

"I wish it had been Great-grace, for their sakes," Hopeful said.

"If it had been, he still might have had his hands full," Christian replied. "For I must tell you that although Great-grace is excellent with his weapons and can do well enough with the thieves as long as he keeps them at sword's length, yet if they get past his guard—even Faint-heart, Mistrust, or the other one—it will be a hard struggle for him not to be thrown to the ground. And when a man is down, you know, what can he do?"

"Anyone who looks closely at Great-grace's face will see the scars and cuts there that prove what I am saying. Yes, I once heard that he said, while he was in combat, 'We were so utterly burdened that we despaired of life itself.[j]' And how those sturdy rogues and their companions made David groan, mourn, and roar! Indeed, Heman and Hezekiah, though champions in their day, were forced to fight for their lives when assaulted by them, and even so, they took a sound beating. Peter, at one time, wanted to see what he could do, but though some say he is the prince of the apostles, they handled him so roughly that they made him afraid of a servant girl.[k]"

"Besides, their king is always at their whistle. He is never out of hearing, and if at any time they are getting the worst of it, he comes in to help them if he can. And of him it is said: 'The sword that touches him cannot prevail, nor the spear, the dart, or the javelin. He counts iron as straw and bronze as rotten wood. The arrow cannot make him flee; for him, sling stones are turned to stubble. Clubs are counted as stubble; he laughs at the rattling of a javelin.[l]' What can a man do in that situation? It is true, if a man could always have Job's horse and had the skill and courage to ride him, he might do remarkable things. For 'its neck is clothed with thunder,' and it is not 'afraid of the grasshopper.' 'The glory of its nostrils is terror. It paws in the valley and exults in its strength; it goes out to meet the weapons. It mocks at fear and is not dismayed; it does not turn back from the sword. Upon it rattle the quiver, the flashing spear, and the javelin. With fierceness and rage it swallows the ground; it cannot stand still at the sound of the trumpet. When the trumpet sounds, it says, 'Aha!' It smells the battle from afar, the thunder of the captains, and the shouting.[m]'"

"But for foot-soldiers like you and me, let us never desire to meet with an enemy, nor boast as if we could do better when we hear of others who have been defeated. And let us not be pleased with the thought of our own strength, for such men commonly get the worst of it when they are tested. Look at Peter, whom I mentioned before. He would brag, yes, he would. He would say, as his vain mind prompted him, that he would do better and stand more firmly for his Master than anyone else. But who else has been so defeated and humiliated by these villains as he was?

Therefore, when we hear that such robberies are done on the King's highway, there are two things we ought to do:

First, to go out fully armed and be sure to take a shield with us. For it was the lack of a shield that prevented the one who struck so powerfully at Leviathan from making him yield. Indeed, if the shield is missing, the enemy does not fear us at all. Therefore, the one who had skill has said, 'In all circumstances take up the shield of faith, with which you can extinguish all the flaming darts of the evil one.[n]'

Second, it is also good that we ask the King for an escort—indeed, that He will go with us Himself. This is what made David rejoice in the

Valley of the Shadow of Death, and Moses would have rather died where he stood than go one step without his God.[o] Oh, my brother, if He will only go along with us, why should we be afraid of ten thousand who set themselves against us?[p] But without Him, the proud helpers 'fall among the slain.'"[q]

"For my part, I have been in the fight before," Christian said. "And though, through the goodness of Him who is best, I am, as you see, still alive, I cannot boast of my own strength. I will be glad if I meet no more such attacks, though I fear we are not yet beyond all danger. However, since the lion and the bear have not yet devoured me, I hope God will also deliver us from the next uncircumcised Philistine." Then Christian sang:

"Poor Little-faith, have you been with the thieves? Were you robbed? Remember this, whoever believes: Get more faith, and a victor you will be Over ten thousand—else, scarce over three."

---

[a] *Pro. 26:12*
[b] *Ecc. 10:3*
[c] *Isa. 27:11*
[d] *Pro. 5:22; Mat 12:45*
[e] *1Pe. 4:18*
[f] *Heb. 12:16*
[g] *Gen. 25:32*
[h] *Jer. 2:24*
[i] *1Pe. 5:8*
[j] *2Co. 1:8*
[k] *Mat. 26:69-72*
[l] *Job. 41:26-29*
[m] *Job. 39:19-25*
[n] *Eph. 6:16*
[o] *Exo. 33:15*
[p] *Psa. 3:5-8; Psa 27:1-3*
[q] *Isa. 10:4*

Chapter 26: The Flatterer and the Net

The Flatterer, a man with robes of light,
Will lead the best of pilgrims from the right.
A whip from God, though painful, sets them free,
A lesson learned in deep humility.

So, they went on, and Ignorance followed. They walked until they came to a place where another path merged with theirs, and it seemed to lie as straight as the path they were supposed to take. They did not know which of the two to choose, for both seemed straight ahead of them. Therefore, they stood still to consider.

And as they were thinking about the way, a man who was black of flesh[1] but covered with a very light robe came to them and asked why they were standing there. They answered that they were going to the Celestial City but did not know which of these paths to take. "Follow me," said the man, "for that is where I am going."

So, they followed him on the path that had just merged with the road. It turned gradually, turning them so far away from the city they desired to go to that, in a short time, their faces were turned away from it, yet they still followed him. Before they knew it, he led them both into a net, in which they were so entangled that they did not know what to do. And with that, the white robe fell from the dark man's back. Then they saw where they were. And so, they lay there for some time, crying, for they could not get themselves out.

Then Christian said to his companion, "Now I see my error. Didn't the Shepherds tell us to beware of the flatterers? As the wise man says, so we have found it to be today: 'A man who flatters his neighbor spreads a net for his feet.[a]'"

---

[1] In Bunyan's 17th-century allegory, the color black is used symbolically to represent a hidden nature of sin and evil, not as a modern racial or ethnic descriptor. The character, the Flatterer, has a "black" (sinful) nature hidden under a "light robe" of false righteousness.

"They also gave us a map with directions for the way, to help us find it more surely," said Hopeful. "But we have forgotten to read it and have not kept ourselves from the paths of the destroyer. In this, David was wiser than we were, for he said, 'By the word of your lips I have avoided the ways of the violent.[b]' "

And so, they lay there, mourning their situation in the net.

At last, they saw a Shining One coming toward them with a whip of small cords in his hand. When he came to where they were, he asked them where they came from and what they were doing there.

They told him that they were poor pilgrims going to Zion but had been led out of their way by a man, black of flesh and clothed in white, "who told us," they said, "to follow him, for he was going there too."

Then the one with the whip said, "He is the Flatterer, a false apostle who has transformed himself into an angel of light.[c]" With that, he tore the net and let the men out. Then he said to them, "Follow me, so that I may set you on your way again." So, he led them back to the path they had left to follow the Flatterer.

Then he asked them, "Where did you spend last night?" They said, "With the Shepherds on the Delectable Mountains." He then asked them if the Shepherds had not given them a map with directions for the way. They answered, "Yes." "And did you," he asked, "pull out your map and consult it when you were stopped and uncertain?" They answered, "No." He asked them, "Why?" They said, "We forgot." He also asked if the Shepherds had not told them to beware of the Flatterer. They answered, "Yes, but we did not imagine that this well-spoken man was him."

Then I saw in my dream that he commanded them to lie down. When they did, he punished them severely to teach them the good way in which they should walk.[d] And as he punished them, he said, "'Those whom I love I rebuke and discipline. So be earnest and repent.'"[e] After this was done, he told them to go on their way and to pay close attention to the other directions of the Shepherds. So, they thanked him for all his kindness and went quietly along the right path, singing:

"Come here, you who walk along the way,
See how the pilgrims fare who go astray.
They are caught within an entangling net,
Because good counsel they too soon forget.
It's true they were rescued, but yet you see,
They're whipped as well. Let this your warning be."

---

[a] *Pro. 29:5*
[b] *Psa. 17:4*
[c] *Pro. 29:5; Dan 11:32; 2 Co 11:13-14*
[d] *Deu. 25:2*
[e] *Rev. 3:19; 2 Ch 6:26-27*

Chapter 27: The Encounter with Atheist

Now at this path I don't know what to say,
If pilgrims find it, they will lose their way.
But if they lose it, and they find it not,
They'll find a whipping and a painful spot.

Now, after a while, they saw someone in the distance coming quietly and alone along the highway to meet them. Then Christian said to his companion, "Over there is a man with his back to Zion, and he is coming to meet us."

"I see him," said Hopeful. "Let's be on guard now, in case he also turns out to be a flatterer." The man drew nearer and nearer and at last came up to them. His name was **Atheist**, and he asked them where they were going.

"We are going to Mount Zion," Christian said.

Then Atheist burst into a great fit of laughter.

"What is the meaning of your laughter?" Christian asked.

"I laugh when I see what ignorant people you are, to take on such a tedious journey when you are likely to get nothing for your troubles but the journey itself," said Atheist.

"Why, man? Do you think we will not be received?" Christian asked.

"Received!" Atheist scoffed. "There is no such place as you dream of in all this world."

"But there is in the world to come," Christian replied.

"I too believed when I was at home. If I had not, I would not have come this far to seek it," Atheist replied. "But since I have found nothing—and I should have found it if such a place existed, for I have gone farther than you to seek it—I am going back again. I plan to enjoy myself with the things I once foolishly threw away while seeking hope in something that, I now see, does not exist."

Then Christian said to his companion Hopeful, "Is what this man has said true?"

"Be careful! He is one of the flatterers," Hopeful replied. "Remember what it cost us once already for listening to this kind of person. What, no Mount Zion? Didn't we see the gate of the City from the Delectable Mountains? Also, are we not supposed to walk by faith now? Let us go on," said Hopeful, "so that the man with the whip does not overtake us again.

"My brother, this is a lesson you should be teaching me, but since you are hesitating, allow me to remind you of it: 'Cease to hear instruction, my son, and you will wander from the words of knowledge.[a]' I am telling you, brother, we must stop listening to him and instead have a faith that saves the soul."[b]

"My brother," Christian said, "I wasn't asking because I was doubting our belief myself, but to test you and to see the honest conviction of your heart. As for this man, I know he is blinded by the god of this world. Let us go on, knowing that we believe the truth, and that 'no lie is of the truth.'"[c]

"Now I rejoice in the hope of the glory of God," Hopeful replied. So they turned away from the man, and he, laughing at them, went his way.

I saw then in my dream that they went on until they came into a certain country whose air naturally tended to make visitors to this place drowsy. Here, Hopeful began to get very dull and heavy with sleep. He said to Christian, "I am now beginning to grow so drowsy that I can barely keep my eyes open. Let's lie down here and take a nap."

"By no means," said Christian, "for if we sleep, we may never wake up again."

"Why, my brother?" Hopeful asked. "Sleep is sweet to a man who works hard. We will be refreshed if we take a nap."

"Don't you remember that one of the Shepherds told us to beware of the **Enchanted Ground**?" Christian replied. "He meant by that that we should beware of sleeping. 'So then, let us not be like others, who are asleep, but let us be awake and sober.'" [d]

---

[a] *Pro. 19:27*
[b] *Heb. 10:39*
[c] *1Jn. 2:21*
[d] *1Th. 5:6*

Chapter 28: Conversation on the Enchanted Ground

When saints do sleepy grow, let them come hither,
And hear how these two pilgrims talk together:
Yea, let them learn of them, in any wise,
Thus to keep open their drowsy, slumb'ring eyes.
Saints' fellowship, if it be managed well,
Keeps them awake, and that in spite of hell.

"I admit my fault," said Hopeful. "If I had been here alone, I would have run the risk of death by sleeping. I see it is true what the wise man says: 'Two are better than one.'[a] Throughout this journey your company has been a mercy to me, and you will have a good reward for your effort."

"Now then," said Christian, "to prevent drowsiness in this place, let us begin a good conversation."

"With all my heart," said Hopeful.

"Where should we begin?"

"Where God began with us. But you begin, if you please."

Then Christian began, "First, I will sing you this song:

When saints grow sleepy, let them gather near, And how two pilgrims talk, let them all hear. Yes, let them learn from them in every way, To keep their drowsy, slumbering eyes at bay. Good fellowship, if it is managed well, Keeps saints awake, in spite of all of hell."

"Now, I will ask you a question," Christian said. "How did you first come to think of living the way you do now?"

"Do you mean, how did I first come to care for the good of my soul?" Hopeful asked.

"Yes, that is what I mean."

"For a long time, I continued to delight in the things that were seen and sold at our fair," Hopeful explained. "Things that, I now believe, would have drowned me in damnation and destruction if I had continued in them."

"What things were they?"

"All the treasures and riches of the world," said Hopeful. "I also delighted in rioting, wild parties, drinking, swearing, lying, impurity, breaking the Sabbath, and anything else that tended to destroy the soul. But in the end, by hearing and thinking about divine things—which I heard from you and also from beloved Faithful, who was put to death for his faith and good life in Vanity Fair—I learned that 'the outcome of those things is death,[b]' and that 'because of such things God's wrath comes on those who are disobedient.[c]'"

"And did you immediately fall under the power of this conviction?" Christian asked.

"No," Hopeful said. "I was not immediately willing to acknowledge the evil of sin or the damnation that follows it. When my mind first began to be shaken by the Word, I tried to shut my eyes against its light."

"But what caused you to react that way to the first workings of God's blessed Spirit in you?" Christian asked.

"For several reasons," Hopeful said. "First, I did not realize that this was the work of God in me. I never thought that God begins the conversion of a sinner with an awakening to sin. Second, sin was still very sweet to my flesh, and I was reluctant to leave it. Third, I did not know how to part with my old companions, since I so enjoyed their presence and ways. And fourth, during the hours in which I felt convicted by my sin, I was so troubled and terrified that I could not even bear the memory of them."

"So then, it seems you were sometimes able to push the convicting thoughts out of your mind?" Christian asked.

"Yes, but then they would return, and I would be as bad, or even worse, than I was before," Hopeful replied.

"Why, what was it that brought your sins to mind again?"

"Many things," said Hopeful. "Such as:

If I happened to meet a good man in the street;

If I heard someone reading from the Bible;

If my head began to ache;

If I was told that some of my neighbors were sick;

If I heard the bell toll for someone who had died;

If I thought of dying myself;

If I heard that sudden death had happened to others;

But especially, when I thought about how I must soon face judgment."

"And were you ever able to shake off the guilt of sin when it came upon you in any of these ways?" Christian asked.

"No, not at all," said Hopeful. "The more I tried to ignore it, the tighter it would grip my conscience. And if I even thought of going back to sin—though my mind was now turned against it—it would be a double torment to me."

"And what did you do then?"

"I thought I must try to mend my life," Hopeful said, "for otherwise, I thought, I am sure to be damned."

"And did you try to mend your ways?" Christian asked.

"Yes," Hopeful said, "I fled not only from my sins but from sinful company, too. I devoted myself to religious duties like prayer, reading, weeping for sin, and speaking truth to my neighbors. I did these things, and many others too numerous to mention here."

"And did you think you were doing well then?"

"Yes, for a while," Hopeful answered. "But in the end, my trouble came tumbling down on me again, right on top of all my efforts to reform."

"How did that happen, since you were now reformed?" Christian asked.

"Several things brought it on," Hopeful said, "especially sayings like these: 'All our righteous acts are like filthy rags.[d]' 'No one will be declared righteous in God's sight by the works of the law.[e]' And, 'When you have done everything you were told to do, you should say, "We are unworthy servants."'[f] From these, I began to reason with myself: If ALL my righteous acts are like filthy rags, if by the works of the law NO ONE can be justified, and if, when we have done EVERYTHING, we are still unworthy, then it is foolish to think I can get to heaven through good works and righteous living.

I also had this thought: If a man runs up a hundred-pound debt with a shopkeeper and after that pays for everything new that he gets, the old debt still remains in the book. For that old debt, the shopkeeper can sue him and have him thrown in prison until he pays it."

"Well, and how did you apply this to yourself?" Christian asked.

"Why, I thought to myself," said Hopeful, "that by my sins I have run up a great debt in God's book, and my current efforts to reform will not pay off that score. Therefore, even with all my present improvements, I still had to ask: How will I be freed from the damnation I have brought upon myself by my past sins?"

"A very good application," said Christian. "But please, go on."

"Another thing that has troubled me, even since my recent improvements, is that if I look closely at the best of what I do now, I still see sin–new sin–mixing itself with the best of my actions," Hopeful said. "So now I am forced to conclude that despite my former high opinion of myself and my good works, I have committed enough sin while carrying out even a single duty to send me to hell, even if my former life had been faultless."

"And what did you do then?" Christian asked.

"What could I do?" Hopeful replied. "I did not know what to do until I shared my thoughts with Faithful, for he and I were well acquainted. He told me that unless I could obtain the righteousness of a man who had never sinned, neither my own righteousness nor all the righteousness of the world could save me."

"And did you think he was telling the truth?" Christian asked.

"If he had told me that when I was pleased and satisfied with my own improvements, I would have called him a fool for his trouble," Hopeful said. "But since I now see my own weakness and the sin that corrupts even my best efforts, I have been forced to agree with his opinion."

"But when he first suggested it to you, did you think such a man could be found, of whom it could be justly said that he never committed sin?" Christian asked.

"I must confess the idea sounded strange at first," Hopeful said, "but after talking with him a little more, I was fully convinced."

"And did you ask him who this man was and how you could be justified by him?"

"Yes," Hopeful said, "and he told me it was the Lord Jesus, who dwells at the right hand of the Most High. 'And this is how you must be justified by Him,' he said, 'by trusting in what He has done Himself, in the days of His flesh, and what He suffered when He hung on the tree.' I asked him further how that man's righteousness could be powerful enough to justify another person before God. And he told me that He was the mighty God,[g] and that He did what He did and also died the death not for Himself, but for me, and that His deeds and their value would be counted as mine if I believed in Him.[h]"

"And what did you do then?" Christian asked.

"I made objections against my own believing, because I thought He was not willing to save me," Hopeful said.

"And what did Faithful say to you then?"

"He told me to go to Him and see. I said that would be presumptuous, but he said no, because I was invited to come.[i] Then he gave me a book containing the message of Jesus to encourage me to come more freely, and he said that concerning that book, every last letter of it stood firmer than heaven and earth.[j] Then I asked him what I should do when I came, and he told me I must beg on my knees, with all my heart and soul, for the Father to reveal Him to me.[k] I asked him further how I should pray to Him, and he said, 'Go, and you will find Him on a mercy-seat, where He sits all year long to give pardon and forgiveness to those who come.[l]' I told him that I did not know what to say when I came. And he told me to say something like this:

'God, be merciful to me, a sinner, and make me know and believe in Jesus Christ. For I see that if His righteousness did not exist, or if I do not have faith in that righteousness, I am utterly lost. Lord, I have heard that you are a merciful God and have ordained that your Son Jesus Christ should be the Savior of the world. Moreover, I have heard that you are willing to give Him to a poor sinner such as I am (and I am a sinner indeed). Lord, take this opportunity, therefore, and magnify your grace in the salvation of my soul, through your Son Jesus Christ. Amen.'"

"And did you do as you were told?" Christian asked.

"Yes, over and over and over," Hopeful replied.

"And did the Father reveal His Son to you?"

"Not the first time, nor the second, nor the third, nor the fourth, nor the fifth, and not even the sixth time."

"What did you do then?"

"What could I do?" said Hopeful. "I didn't know what to do."

"Didn't you think about giving up on praying?" Christian asked.

"Yes, two hundred times," Hopeful said.

"And what was the reason you did not?"

"I believed that what I had been told was true," Hopeful answered, "that without the righteousness of this Christ, the whole world could not save me. And so I thought to myself, 'If I give up, I will die, and the best place to die is at the throne of grace.' And at the same time, this came into my mind: 'Though it linger, wait for it; it will certainly come and will not delay.' So I continued praying until the Father showed me His Son."

"And how was He revealed to you?" Christian asked.

"I did not see Him with my physical eyes, but with the eyes of my understanding," Hopeful said. "This is how it happened: One day I was very sad—sadder, I think, than at any other time in my life—and this sadness came from a fresh realization of the greatness and wickedness of my sins. And as I was expecting nothing but hell and the everlasting damnation of my soul, suddenly, in my mind's eye, I saw the Lord Jesus Christ look down from heaven upon me and say, 'Believe in the Lord Jesus, and you will be saved.'"[m]

"But I replied, 'Lord, I am a great, a very great sinner.' And He answered, 'My grace is sufficient for you.'[n] Then I said, 'But Lord, what is believing?' And then I understood from that saying, 'Whoever comes to me shall not hunger, and whoever believes in me shall never thirst,' that believing and coming were the same thing, and that the one who came—that is, the one who ran with his whole heart and his affections toward salvation by Christ—was the one who truly believed in Christ.[o]"

"Then tears welled up in my eyes, and I asked further, 'But Lord, can a sinner as great as I am truly be accepted and saved by you?' And I heard Him say, 'Whoever comes to me I will never cast out.[p]' Then I said, 'But Lord, how must I think of you when I come to you, so that my faith may be rightly placed in you?'

Then He said, 'Christ Jesus came into the world to save sinners.[q]' 'He is the culmination of the law so that there may be righteousness for everyone who believes.[r]' 'He was delivered over to death for our sins and was raised to life for our justification.[s]' 'He loves us and has freed us from our sins by his blood.[t]' 'He is the one mediator between God and mankind.[u]' And, 'He always lives to intercede for them.[v]'"

"From all this, I gathered that I must look for righteousness in His person and for payment for my sins through His blood," Hopeful said. "I understood that what He did in obedience to His Father's law, and in submitting to its penalty, was not for Himself but for anyone who will accept it for their salvation and be thankful. And now my heart was full of joy, my eyes were full of tears, and my affections were overflowing with love for the name, people, and ways of Jesus Christ."

"This was truly a revelation of Christ to your soul," Christian said. "But tell me, specifically, what effect this had on your spirit."

"It made me see that the whole world, despite all its righteousness, is in a state of condemnation," Hopeful replied. "It made me see how God the Father, without compromising His own justice, could righteously declare a coming sinner 'not guilty.' It made me greatly ashamed of the wickedness of my former life and overwhelmed me with a sense of my own ignorance, for no thought had ever come into my heart before that showed me the beauty of Jesus Christ in this way. It made me love a holy life and long to do something for the honor and glory of the name of the Lord Jesus. Indeed, I thought that if I had a thousand gallons of blood in my body, I could spill it all for the sake of the Lord Jesus."

---

[a] *Ecc. 4:9*
[b] *Rom. 6:21*
[c] *Eph. 5:6*
[d] *Isa. 64:6*
[e] *Gal. 2:16*
[f] *Luk. 17:10*
[g] *Rom. 9:5*
[h] *1Pe. 1:21*
[i] *Mat. 11:28*
[j] *Mat. 24:35*
[k] *Psa. 95:6; Dan 6:10; Jer 29:12-13*
[l] *Exo. 25:22; Lev 16:2; Heb 4:16*
[m] *Act. 16:31*
[n] *2Co. 12:9*
[o] *Jhn. 6:35*
[p] *Jhn. 6:37*
[q] *1Ti. 1:15*
[r] *Rom. 10:4*
[s] *Rom. 4:25*
[t] *Rev. 1:5*
[u] *1Ti. 2:5*
[v] *Heb. 7:25*

Chapter 29: The Case of Ignorance

The man of conceit will find his final fall,
Though on the name of Jesus he may call;
He enters not the gate, but climbs the wall,
And so is doomed to perish, once for all.

I saw then in my dream that Hopeful looked back and saw Ignorance, whom they had left behind, coming after them. "Look," he said to Christian, "see how far that young man is lagging behind."

"Yes, yes, I see him," Christian replied. "He does not care for our company."

"I think he would have benefited from remaining in our company all this time," said Hopeful.

"That is true," said Christian, "but I guarantee you he thinks otherwise."

"I think he does," Hopeful agreed. "But nevertheless, let's wait for him." So they did.

Then Christian said to him, "Come on, man, why are you lagging so far behind?"

"I take more pleasure in walking alone than in company, unless I happen to like the company," Ignorance replied.

Then Christian said to Hopeful softly, "Didn't I tell you he doesn't care for our company? But in any case, let's come together and talk to pass the time in this lonely place." Then, directing his speech to Ignorance, he said, "Come, how are you doing? How do things stand between God and your soul now?"

"I hope all is well," Ignorance said, "for I am always full of good impulses that come into my mind to comfort me as I walk."

"What good impulses?" Christian asked. "Please, tell us."

"Why, I think of God and heaven," Ignorance answered.

"So do the devils and the damned souls," Christian replied.

"But I think of them and also desire them," said Ignorance.

"So do many who are never likely to get there," Christian replied. "'The soul of the sluggard craves and gets nothing.[a]'"

"But I think of them and leave everything for them."

"I doubt that," Christian said, "for leaving everything is a hard thing to do—yes, harder than many people realize. But why, and by what, are you persuaded that you have left everything for God and heaven?"

"My heart tells me so," Ignorance answered.

"The wise man says, 'Whoever trusts in his own mind is a fool,[b]'" Christian replied.

"That is spoken of an evil heart," said Ignorance, "but mine is a good one."

"And how do you prove that?"

"It comforts me with the hope of heaven," Ignorance said.

"That may be due to its deceitfulness," said Christian, "for a person's heart can give him comfort in the hope of something for which he has no reason to hope."

"But my heart and my life are in agreement," Ignorance insisted, "and therefore my hope is well-founded."

"Who told you that your heart and your life are in agreement?"

"My heart tells me so."

"'Ask my accomplice if I am a thief!'" Christian shot back. "Your heart tells you so? Unless the Word of God testifies in this matter, any other testimony is worthless."

"But isn't it a good heart that has good thoughts?" Ignorance asked. "And isn't it a good life that is in accordance with God's commandments?"

"Yes, a heart that has good thoughts is a good heart, and a life that is in accordance with God's commandments is a good life," Christian replied. "But it is one thing to actually have them, and another thing entirely to only *think* you have them."

"Please, what do you consider good thoughts, and a life in accordance with God's commandments?" Ignorance asked.

"There are good thoughts of many kinds," Christian said. "Some concern ourselves, some concern God, some concern Christ, and some concern other things."

"What are good thoughts concerning ourselves?" Ignorance asked.

"Those that agree with the Word of God," Christian answered.

"When do our thoughts about ourselves agree with the Word of God?"

"When we pass the same judgment on ourselves that the Word passes on us," Christian said. "Let me explain. The Word of God says of people in their natural condition, 'There is no one righteous, not even one; there is no one who does good.[c]' It also says that 'every inclination of the thoughts of the human heart was only evil all the time.[d]' And again, 'every inclination of his heart is evil from childhood.[e]' Now then, when we think of ourselves in this way, and truly feel it, then our thoughts are good, because they are in agreement with the Word of God."

"I will never believe that my heart is that bad," Ignorance declared.

"Therefore, you have never had a single good thought about yourself in your entire life," Christian replied. "But let me continue. Just as the Word passes judgment on our hearts, it also passes judgment on our ways. When our thoughts about our hearts and our ways agree with the judgment that the Word gives on both, then our thoughts are good, because they are in agreement with it."

"Explain what you mean," said Ignorance.

"Well, the Word of God says that man's ways are crooked—not good, but perverse,[f]" Christian said. "It says that people are naturally off the good path and have never known it.[g] Now, when a person thinks of their ways in this manner—I mean, when they think this way with true feeling and a humble heart—then they have good thoughts about their own ways, because their thoughts now agree with the judgment of the Word of God."

"What are good thoughts concerning God?" Ignorance asked.

"Just as I have said concerning ourselves: when our thoughts about God agree with what the Word says about Him," Christian replied. "That is, when we think of His being and His attributes as the Word has taught, which I cannot discuss at length right now. But to speak of Him in reference to us, we have right thoughts about God when we think that He knows us better than we know ourselves and can see sin in us when and where we can see none in ourselves. When we think that He knows our inmost thoughts and that our heart, with all its depths, is always open to His eyes. And also, when we think that all our righteous acts stink in His nostrils, and that therefore He cannot bear to see us stand before Him with any confidence, even in our best performances."

"Do you think I am such a fool as to believe God cannot see further than I can?" Ignorance demanded. "Or that I would come to God trusting in my own best performances?"

"Well, what do you think about this matter?" Christian asked.

"To be brief," said Ignorance, "I think I must believe in Christ for my justification."

"How can you say you must believe in Christ when you don't see your need for Him?" Christian challenged. "You see neither your original sin nor your actual weaknesses. Instead, you have such a high opinion of yourself and of what you do that it plainly shows you have never seen the necessity of Christ's personal righteousness to justify you before God. How, then, can you say, 'I believe in Christ'?"

"I believe well enough, regardless of all that," said Ignorance.

"How do you believe?" Christian asked.

"I believe that Christ died for sinners and that I will be justified before God from the curse through His gracious acceptance of my obedience to His law," Ignorance said. "Or, to put it another way, Christ makes my religious duties acceptable to His Father because of His merits, and in that way, I will be justified."

"Let me give an answer to this confession of your faith," Christian said.

"First, you believe with a fantasy faith, for this kind of faith is described nowhere in the Word.

Second, you believe with a false faith because it takes justification away from the personal righteousness of Christ and applies it to your own.

Third, this faith does not make Christ a justifier of your person, but only of your actions—and it justifies your person only for the sake of your actions, which is false.

Fourth, therefore, this faith is deceitful and will leave you under God's wrath on the day of judgment.

True, justifying faith causes the soul, being aware of its hopeless condition under the law, to fly for refuge to Christ's righteousness. This righteousness is not an act of grace by which He makes your own obedience acceptable to God for justification. Rather, it is His personal obedience to the law—His doing and suffering on our behalf what the law required of us. This is the righteousness that true faith accepts. Sheltered under it, the soul is presented as spotless before God, accepted, and cleared of all condemnation."

"What! You want us to trust in what Christ has done in His own person, without us?" Ignorance scoffed. "This idea would loosen the reins on our desires and allow us to live however we please. For what does it matter how we live, if we can be justified from everything by Christ's personal righteousness, just by believing it?"

"Ignorance is your name, and your nature is just like your name," Christian said. "Even this answer proves what I am saying. You are ignorant of what justifying righteousness is, and you are just as ignorant of how to secure your soul from the heavy wrath of God through faith in it. Yes, and you are also ignorant of the true effects of saving faith in this righteousness of Christ, which is to bow and win over the heart to God in Christ, to love His name, His Word, His ways, and His people—and not to live as you ignorantly imagine."

"Ask him if he has ever had Christ revealed to him from heaven," Hopeful suggested.

"What!" Ignorance exclaimed. "You are a man who believes in revelations! I believe that what you and all the rest of your kind say about that matter is just the fruit of confused minds."

"Why, man!" Hopeful replied. "Christ is so hidden from the natural understanding of human beings that no one can know Him in a saving way unless God the Father reveals Him to them."

"That is your faith, but not mine," said Ignorance. "Yet I have no doubt that my faith is as good as yours, even though I don't have as many fantasies in my head as you do."

"Allow me to add a word," Christian said. "You should not speak so lightly of this matter. For I will boldly declare, just as my good companion has done, that no one can know Jesus Christ except by the revelation of the Father.[h] Yes, and true faith as well—the faith by which the soul takes hold of Christ—must be created by the exceeding greatness of His mighty power.[i] I can see, poor Ignorance, that you are ignorant of the working of this faith. Be awakened, then! See your own wretchedness and fly to the Lord Jesus. By His righteousness—which is the righteousness of God, for He Himself is God—you shall be delivered from condemnation.[j]"

"You go too fast; I cannot keep pace with you," said Ignorance. "You go on ahead. I must stay a while behind." Then they said:

"Well, Ignorance, will you still foolish be,
To scorn good counsel, given ten times to thee?
And if you still refuse it, you will know,
Before too long, the evil that you sow.
Remember, man, in time, bow down, don't fear;
Good counsel, taken well, saves you, so hear.
But if you still should scorn it, you will be
The loser, Ignorance, I guarantee."

Then Christian said to his companion, "Well, come on, my good Hopeful. I see that you and I must walk by ourselves again."

---

[a] *Pro. 13:4*
[b] *Pro. 28:26*
[c] *Rom. 3:10-12*
[d] *Gen. 6:5*
[e] *Gen. 8:21*
[f] *Psa. 125:5; Pro 2:15*
[g] *Rom. 3:12*
[h] *Mat. 11:27*
[i] *Eph. 1:18-19*
[j] *2Co. 5:21*

Chapter 30: The Nature of Right Fear

"Indeed, the Word says, 'He has blinded their eyes, so that they cannot see,[a]'" Christian replied. "But now that we are by ourselves, what do you think of such men? Do you think they never have convictions of sin, and therefore never fear that their state is dangerous?"

"It is best for you to answer that question yourself, for you are the more mature believer," Hopeful said.

"Then I will speculate that they may feel convicted sometimes," Christian answered, "but being naturally ignorant, they do not understand that such convictions are for their own good. As a result, they desperately try to suppress them, and they flatter themselves about the goodness of their own hearts."

"I believe, as you say, that such fear works for a person's good and helps set them on the right path when they are beginning their pilgrimage," said Hopeful.

"Without a doubt it does, if it is the right kind of fear," Christian replied. "For the Word says, 'The fear of the LORD is the beginning of wisdom.[b]'"

"How would you describe the right kind of fear?" Hopeful asked.

"True or right fear is recognized by three things," Christian said.

"First, by its source: it is caused by a recognition of the sin that separates us from God.

Second, it drives the soul to take firm hold of Christ for salvation.

Third, it creates in the soul a sustained reverence for God, His Word, and His ways. It keeps the soul tender and makes it afraid to turn from them to the right or to the left, or to do anything that might dishonor God, break its peace, grieve the Spirit, or give the enemy a reason to accuse us."

"Well said. I believe you have spoken the truth," Hopeful replied. "Are we almost past the Enchanted Ground now?"

"Why, are you tired of this conversation?" Christian asked.

"No, not at all, but I would like to know where we are."

"We only have about two more miles to go on it," Christian said. "But let's return to our subject. The ignorant do not know that these convictions which cause them to be afraid are working for their good, and so they try to suppress them."

"How do they try to suppress them?" Hopeful asked.

"First, because they think that these fears are created by the devil (though they are actually created by God), they resist them like they would other sinful thoughts," Christian explained. "Second, they think that these fears threaten their faith, when, alas for these poor men, they have no faith at all! And so, they harden their hearts against them. Third, they presume that they ought not to fear, and therefore, in defiance of their fears, they embrace a superficial confidence. Fourth, they recognize that these fears threaten their pathetic old self-righteousness, and so they resist them with all their might."

"I know something of this myself," said Hopeful, "for before I truly knew myself, it was the same with me."

---

[a] *Isa. 6:9-10; Jhn 12:40*
[b] *Job. 28:28; Psa 111:10; Pro 1:7; Pro 9:10*

Chapter 31: The Story of Temporary

Some start the path but turn and fall away,
Mistaking feelings for the light of day.
A shallow faith that has no root in grace,
Will wither when it finds a harder place.

"Well, for now, let's leave our neighbor Ignorance to himself and take up another beneficial subject," Christian said.

"I would be delighted," said Hopeful, "but you must begin."

"Alright then," said Christian. "Did you happen to know, about ten years ago, a man in your area named **Temporary**, who was very enthusiastic about religion?"

"Know him? Yes," Hopeful replied. "He lived in **Graceless**, a town about two miles from **Honesty**, and he lived next door to a man named **Turn-back**."

"Correct, he lived under the same roof with him," Christian said. "Well, that man had a great awakening once. I believe that at that time he had some awareness of his sins and of the wages that were due for them."

"I agree with you," said Hopeful, "for, since my house was not more than three miles from his, he would often come to me, and with many tears. Truly, I pitied the man and was not entirely without hope for him. But as you can see, not everyone who cries, 'Lord, Lord,' is sincere."

"He told me once that he was determined to go on pilgrimage, just as we are now," Christian said. "But all of a sudden, he became acquainted with a man named **Save-self**, and after that, he no longer associated with me."

"Since we are talking about him," said Hopeful, "let's explore the reason why he and others like him suddenly backslide into their old lives."

"That could be very beneficial," Christian said, "but you begin."

"Well then, in my judgment, there are four reasons for it," Hopeful began.

"First, although the consciences of such men are awakened, their minds are not truly changed. So, when the power of their guilt wears away, the thing that provoked them to be religious is gone, and they naturally turn back to their old ways. It is just like a dog that is sick from something it has eaten. As long as the sickness lasts, it vomits everything up, not because it has a will to do so, but because its stomach is troubled. But when the sickness is over and its stomach is settled, its desire for its own vomit has not gone away, so it turns around and licks it all up again. And so what the scripture says is true, 'The dog returns to its own vomit.[a]' In the same way, these men are passionate for heaven only because of their fear of the torments of hell. As their sense of hell and their fear of damnation cool off, so do their desires for heaven and salvation. So, when their guilt and fear are gone, their desires for heaven and happiness die, and they return to their old ways."

"Second, they have worldly fears that overpower them. I am speaking now of the fear of men, for 'the fear of man lays a snare.[b]' So then, although they seem to be passionate for heaven as long as the flames of hell are licking at their ears, when that terror has subsided a little, they have second thoughts. They begin to think it is good to be wise and not to risk losing everything—or at least, bringing themselves into unavoidable and unnecessary trouble. And so they fall in line with the world again."

"Third, the shame that comes with religion is also a stumbling block in their path. They are proud and arrogant, and in their eyes, religion is a low and contemptible thing. Therefore, when they have lost their immediate sense of hell and the wrath to come, they return to their ways.

Fourth, guilt and meditating on terror are painful to them. They do not like to imagine their future misery before they are in it, (though perhaps seeing it now, if they were willing to look, would make them flee to where the righteous flee and are safe). But because they, as I hinted before, avoid the very thoughts of guilt and terror, once those early awakenings about the terrors and wrath of God subside, they gladly harden their hearts and choose paths that will harden them even more."

"You have gotten very close to the heart of the matter," said Christian, "for the root of it all is the lack of a true change in their mind and will. They are just like the felon who stands before the judge: he quakes and trembles and seems to repent most genuinely, but the real reason is his fear of the noose. It is not that he has any hatred for his crime, which becomes obvious the moment he is set free because he will go right back to being a thief and a rogue. If his mind were truly changed, however, he would be a different person."

"Now that I have described the reasons they go back," said Hopeful, "can you describe the process by which it happens?"

"Of course," Christian replied.

"First, they turn their thoughts away, as much as they can, from any thoughts of God, death, and the judgment to come."

"Second, they gradually cast-off private duties, like private prayer, curbing their desires, being watchful, feeling sorrow for sin, and things like that.

Third, they avoid the company of lively and passionate Christians.

Fourth, after that, they grow cold toward public duties, like hearing sermons, reading, godly conversation, and so on.

Fifth, they then begin to 'pick holes,' as we say, in the coats of some of the godly, finding examples of hypocrisy or personal failure. They do this devilishly, so that they may have a seemingly good reason to throw religion behind their backs, all justified by some weakness they have spotted in others.

Sixth, they then begin to cling to and associate with worldly, loose, and wicked people.

Seventh, they then give in to worldly and wicked conversations in secret, and they are glad if they can see such behavior in anyone who is considered honest, so that they can do it more boldly by following their example.

Eighth, after this, they begin to play with little sins openly.

Ninth, and then, being hardened, they show themselves for what they truly are. In this way, they are launched again into the gulf of misery, and unless a miracle of grace prevents it, they will perish everlastingly in their own self-deception."

---

[a] *2Pe. 2:22*
[b] *Pro. 29:25*

Chapter 32: The Land of Beulah

The pilgrims now, beyond the reach of dread,
Approach the city where the saints are led.
The air is sweet, the sun shines night and day,
And Shining Ones come out to guide their way.

Now I saw in my dream that by this time the pilgrims had crossed over the Enchanted Ground and were entering the country of **Beulah**.[1] The air there was very sweet and pleasant, and since the path lay directly through it, they rested and refreshed themselves there for a season. Here they continually heard the singing of birds, saw the flowers appear on the earth every day, and heard the voice of the turtledove in the land.[a] In this country, the sun shines night and day. This place was beyond the Valley of the Shadow of Death and also out of the reach of Giant Despair; from this place, they could not even see Doubting Castle.

Here they were within sight of their destination. They were also met by some of the City's inhabitants, for in this land, the Shining Ones commonly walked because it was on the borders of heaven. In this land, the contract between the bride and the bridegroom was also renewed. Yes, here, "As a bridegroom rejoices over his bride, so will your God rejoice over you.[b]" Here they had no lack of grain and wine, for in this place they found an abundance of what they had sought throughout their pilgrimage.[c] Here they heard loud voices from out of the City, calling, "'Say to Daughter Zion, "See, your Savior comes! See, his reward is with him."' And here all the inhabitants of the country called them 'The Holy People,' 'The Redeemed of the LORD,' and 'Sought After.'"[d]

Now as they walked in this land, they rejoiced more than they did during any of the earlier parts of their journey, when they were farther

---

[1] *"Beulah" is a Hebrew name for the land of Israel taken from the prophet Isaiah, meaning "married." This land represents the joyful, intimate state of a mature believer who is on the very border of heaven, fully assured of Christ's love and secure in their relationship with Him.*

from the kingdom to which they were bound. As they drew nearer to the City, they had an even clearer view of it. It was built of pearls and precious stones, and its streets were paved with gold. Because of the natural glory of the City and the reflection of the sun on it, Christian grew sick with longing. Hopeful also had a fit or two of the same sickness. Therefore, they lay down for a while, crying out from the pain of longing, "If you find my beloved, tell him I am faint with love.[e]"

But, feeling a little stronger and better able to bear their sickness, they walked on their way and came nearer and nearer to a place with orchards, vineyards, and gardens, whose gates opened onto the highway. As they came up to these places, the gardener was standing in the path. The pilgrims said to him, "Whose lovely vineyards and gardens are these?"

He answered, "They are the King's and are planted here for His own delight and also for the comfort of pilgrims." So the gardener brought them into the vineyards and told them to refresh themselves with the delicacies.[f] He also showed them the King's walking paths and the arbors where He delighted to be, and they stayed there and slept.

Now I saw in my dream that at this time, they talked more in their sleep than they ever did on their entire journey. As I was wondering about this, the gardener said to me, "Why are you surprised? It is the nature of the fruit of the grapes in these vineyards to go down so sweetly that it causes the lips of those who are asleep to speak.[g]"

---

[a] *Son. 2:10-12*
[b] *Isa. 62:5*
[c] *Isa. 62:8-9*
[d] *Isa. 62:11-12*
[e] *Son. 5:8*
[f] *Deu. 23:24*
[g] *Son. 7:9*

Chapter 33: The River of Death

So, I saw that when they awoke, they prepared to go up to the City. But as I said, the reflection of the sun on the City (for the City was pure gold)[a] was so intensely glorious that they could not yet look at it with an unveiled face, but only through an instrument made for that purpose. And I saw that as they went on, two men met them in clothing that shone like gold, and their faces also shone like the light.[b]

These men asked the pilgrims where they came from, and they told them. They also asked them where they had stayed, what difficulties and dangers, and what comforts and pleasures they had met with on the way, and they told them. Then the men who met them said, "You have only two more difficulties to face, and then you will be in the City."

Christian and his companion then asked the men to accompany them, and they agreed. "But," they said, "you must reach the City by your own faith." So, I saw in my dream that they all went on together until they came in sight of the gate.

Now I saw that between them and the gate was a river, but there was no bridge to cross it, and the river was very deep. At the sight of this river, the pilgrims were stunned. But the men who went with them said, "You must go through it, or you cannot get to the gate."

The pilgrims then began to ask if there was another way to the gate. They answered, "Yes, but since the foundation of the world, no one except for two—namely, Enoch and Elijah—has been permitted to walk that path, and no one else will be until the last trumpet sounds.[c]"

The pilgrims, and especially Christian, then began to despair. They looked this way and that, but they could find no way to escape the river. Then they asked the men if the water was all the same depth. "No," they said, "but we cannot help you with that. You will find it deeper or shallower according to your faith in the King of the place."

They turned to face the water. Immediately upon entering, Christian began to sink. Crying out to his good friend Hopeful, he said, "I am sinking in deep waters! The waves are crashing over my head; all your waves have gone over me! Selah.[d]"

Then Hopeful said, "Be cheerful, my brother! I feel the bottom, and it is solid."

"Ah, my friend!" said Christian. "The sorrows of death surround me! I will not see the land that flows with milk and honey." And with that, a great darkness and horror fell upon Christian, so that he could not see in front of him.

Here he also largely lost his senses, so that he could not remember or speak coherently of any of the sweet comforts he had received on his pilgrimage. But all the words he spoke revealed the horror in his mind and the deep fear in his heart that he would die in that river and never enter the gate. Here also, as those standing by could see, he was greatly troubled by thoughts of the sins he had committed, both before and after he began his pilgrimage. It was also observed that he was troubled by visions of hobgoblins and evil spirits, for he would frequently hint at them with his words.

Hopeful struggled to keep his brother's head above water. Sometimes Christian would go down completely, and then a moment later, rise up again half-dead. Hopeful also tried to comfort him:

"Brother, I see the gate, and men standing by to receive us!" said Hopeful.

"It is you, it is you they are waiting for!" answered Christian. "You have been Hopeful ever since I've known you."

"So have you!" Hopeful said to Christian.

"Ah, brother!" Christian cried. "Surely, if I were in the right, He would now rise up to help me. But because of my sins, He has brought me into this trap and has left me."

Then Hopeful said, "My brother, you have completely forgotten the scripture where it says of the wicked, 'For they have no pangs in their death; their bodies are fat and sleek. They are not in trouble as others are; they are not stricken like the rest of mankind.[e]' These troubles and distresses you are going through in these waters are not a sign that God has forsaken you. Instead, they are sent to test you, to see whether you will remember the goodness you have received from Him in the past and live by faith in Him in your distress."

Then I saw in my dream that Christian was lost in thought for a moment. Hopeful then added, "Be cheerful! Jesus Christ makes you whole." With that, Christian cried out with a loud voice, "Oh, I see Him again! And He tells me, 'When you pass through the waters, I will be with you; and when you pass through the rivers, they will not sweep over you.[f]'" Then they both took courage, and after that, the enemy was as still as a stone until they had crossed over. Christian immediately found solid ground to stand on, and the rest of the river was shallow. And so they got across.

---

[a] *Rev. 21:18*
[b] *2Co. 3:18*
[c] *1Co. 15:51-52*
[d] *Psa. 42:7*
[e] *Psa. 73:4-5*
[f] *Isa. 43:2*

Chapter 34: The Celestial City

Now, now, look how the holy pilgrims ride,
Clouds are their chariots, angels are their guide:
Who would not here for him all hazards run,
That thus provides for his when this world's done?

Now, on the bank of the river on the other side, they saw the two shining men again, who were waiting there for them. When the pilgrims came out of the river, the shining ones greeted them, saying, "We are ministering spirits, sent to serve those who will inherit salvation.[a]" And so they all went along toward the gate.

You must note that the City stood on a mighty hill, but the pilgrims went up that hill with ease because they had these two men leading them by the arms. They had also left their mortal clothing behind them in the river, for though they went in with them, they came out without them. So, they climbed with great agility and speed, though the foundation on which the City was built was higher than the clouds. They went up through the regions of the air, talking sweetly as they went, comforted because they had safely crossed the river and had such glorious companions to escort them.

The conversation they had with the Shining Ones was about the glory of the place, and the Shining Ones told them that its beauty and glory were beyond description. "There," they said, "is Mount Zion, the heavenly Jerusalem, the countless company of angels, and the spirits of righteous men made perfect.[b] You are going now to the paradise of God, where you will see the tree of life and eat of its never-fading fruit. And when you arrive, you will be given white robes, and you will walk and talk every day with the King, for all the days of eternity.[c]"

"There you will never again see the things you saw in the lower region on the earth—namely, sorrow, sickness, affliction, and death, for the old things have passed away. You are now going to Abraham, to Isaac, and to Jacob, and to the prophets—men whom God has taken away from the evil to come, and who are now at rest, each one walking in his righteousness.[d]"

Then the pilgrims asked, "What must we do in the holy place?"

To which they were answered, "There you will receive comfort for all your toil and have joy for all your sorrow. You must reap what you have sown[e]—the very fruit of all your prayers, tears, and sufferings for the King along the way. In that place, you will wear crowns of gold and enjoy the perpetual sight and vision of the Holy One, for there you will see Him as He is.[f]"

"There you will also serve Him continually with praise, shouting, and thanksgiving—the one you desired to serve when you were in the world (though you found it terribly difficult because of the weakness of your flesh). There your eyes will be delighted with seeing, and your ears with hearing the pleasant voice of the Mighty One. There you will enjoy your friends again who have gone there before you, and there you will joyfully receive every single person who follows you into the holy place.

There you will also be clothed with glory and majesty and be given equipment fit to ride out with the King of Glory. When He comes with the sound of a trumpet in the clouds, as if on the wings of the wind, you will come with Him. When He sits on the throne of judgment, you will sit by Him. Yes, and when He passes sentence on all the workers of evil, whether they are angels or men, you will also have a voice in that judgment, because they were His enemies and yours.[g] Also, when He returns again to the City, you will go too, with the sound of a trumpet, and be with Him forever."

Now, while they were drawing near to the gate, a company of the heavenly host came out to meet them. The two Shining Ones said to the host, "These are the men who loved our Lord when they were in the world and have left everything for His holy name. He has sent us to bring them, and we have brought them this far on their desired journey so that they may go in and look their Redeemer in the face with joy."

Then the heavenly host gave a great shout, saying, "Blessed are those who are invited to the wedding supper of the Lamb![h]"

At this time, several of the King's trumpeters also came out to meet them. They were clothed in white and shining garments and, with loud and melodious music, they made the very heavens echo with their sound. These trumpeters greeted Christian and his companion with ten thousand welcomes from the world they had left, and they did this with shouting and the sound of trumpets.

After this, they surrounded the pilgrims on every side. Some went before, some behind, some on the right, and some on the left (as if to guard them through the upper regions), continually playing their melodious music in high notes as they went. The very sight of it, for those who could see it, was as if heaven itself had come down to meet them.

And so they walked on together. As they walked, the trumpeters would frequently, with a joyful sound, mix their music with looks and gestures to show Christian and his brother how welcome they were in their company and with what gladness they had come to meet them. Now these two men were, in a sense, in heaven before they even arrived, being completely overwhelmed by the sight of angels and the sound of their melodious music. Here they also had the City itself in view, and they thought they heard all its bells ringing to welcome them. But above all were the warm and joyful thoughts they had about their own home there, with such company, forever and ever. Oh, what tongue or pen can express their glorious joy! And so, they came up to the gate.

Now, when they had come up to the gate, this was written over it in letters of gold: "Blessed are those who wash their robes, so that they may have the right to the tree of life and may enter the city by its gates.[i]"

Then I saw in my dream that the Shining Ones told them to call at the gate. When they did, several figures looked down from above the gate—namely, Enoch, Moses, and Elijah. Someone said to them, "These pilgrims have come from the City of Destruction because of the love they have for the King of this place." Then the pilgrims each gave them the **scroll**[1] that they had received at the beginning of their journey. These were then carried in to the King, who, after reading them, said, "Where

---

1 As explained in the note for Chapter 5, this scroll (or certification) represents the assurance of salvation. Here, at the final gate, its importance is fully revealed: it serves as the necessary evidence of a genuine, faith-based righteousness in Christ, which is the only valid pass for entry into heaven. Ignorance's lack of a certificate is the ultimate proof that his own good works and self-righteousness were worthless.

are the men?" To which it was answered, "They are standing outside the gate." The King then commanded the gate to be opened, saying, "Open the gates, that the righteous nation that keeps faith may enter in.[j]"

Now I saw in my dream that these two men went in at the gate, and as they entered, they were transfigured, and they were given clothing that shone like gold. There were also those who met them with harps and crowns and gave them to the pilgrims—the harps for praising and the crowns as a token of honor. Then I heard in my dream that all the bells in the City rang again for joy and that it was said to them, "ENTER INTO THE JOY OF YOUR LORD.[k]" I also heard the men themselves sing with a loud voice, saying, "TO HIM WHO SITS ON THE THRONE AND TO THE LAMB BE PRAISE AND HONOR AND GLORY AND POWER, FOR EVER AND EVER![l]"

Now, just as the gates were opened to let the men in, I looked in after them and saw that the City shone like the sun. Its streets were also paved with gold, and walking on them were many men with crowns on their heads, palms in their hands, and golden harps with which to sing praises.

There were also some who had wings, and they called to one another without ceasing, saying, "Holy, holy, holy is the Lord.[m]" And after that, they shut the gates. When I had seen this, I wished that I myself were among them.

Now, while I was gazing at all these things, I turned my head to look back and saw Ignorance come up to the riverside. He got over it quickly and without half the difficulty faced by the other two men. For it happened that there was a ferryman in that place named **Vain-hope**, who helped him across with his boat. So Ignorance, just as I saw the others do, ascended the hill to come to the gate. Only, he came alone, and no one met him with even the slightest encouragement.

When he had come up to the gate, he looked up at the writing above it and then began to knock, assuming that he would be granted entrance quickly. But the men who looked over the top of the gate asked him, "Where do you come from, and what do you want?"

He answered, "I have eaten and drunk in the presence of the King, and he has taught in our streets.[n]" Then they asked him for his certificate so that they might go in and show it to the King. He fumbled in his shirt for one but found none. Then they said, "You have none?" But the man did not answer.

So, they told the King, but he would not come down to see him. Instead, he commanded the two Shining Ones who had escorted Christian and Hopeful to the City to go out, take Ignorance, and bind him hand and foot and take him away. Then they took him up and carried him through the air to the door that I had seen in the side of the hill, and they put him in there.

Then I saw that there is a way to Hell even from the gates of Heaven, just as there is from the City of Destruction. So, I awoke, and it was a dream.

---

a Heb. 1:14
b Heb. 12:22-24
c Rev. 2:7; Rev 3:4; Rev 22:5
d Isa. 57:1-2; Isa 65:17
e Gal. 6:7
f 1Jn. 3:2
g 1Th. 4:13-17; Jud. 1:14; Dan. 7:9-10; 1Co. 6:2-3
h Rev. 19:9
i Rev. 22:14
j Isa. 26:2
k Mat. 25:23
l Rev. 5:13
m Rev. 4:8
n Luk. 13:26

Made in the USA
Coppell, TX
10 March 2026

73547317R10095